Edited by Stephanie Parent
www.oliviahayle.com

The Billionaire Scrooge Next Door

OLIVIA HAYLE

1 Holly

I return home for the holidays with three goals. Spending time with my family, eating my weight in turkey, and decorating a real-life tree. Not the tiny plastic one I have in my too-small city apartment. No, a real one, bought at the Fairhill Christmas Tree Market like always.

I want our dog nibbling at my shoes and my parents bickering softly about how to cook the turkey. I want my loud and obnoxious brother to be loud and obnoxious again, and not the way he is around his fiancée, which is unfailingly polite and big-brotherly and calm.

What I want is to time travel to past-me.

When life was easy, when I had high hopes, when the world was my oyster. In other words, far away from who I am now. Just another twenty-nine-year-old, a burned-out millennial with credit card debt and a master's degree that promised more than it delivered.

But Fairhill is always the same.

It's always supposed to stay the same.

This year, however, Fairhill is not co-operating. It starts when Mom picks me up at the bus stop. We're driving through the quiet, snowy city when I spot the first sign of disaster.

"What are they doing to the old art center?" I ask. The windows are empty and dark, the door boarded shut.

"Oh, it's being turned into strip mall."

"A strip mall? What about the old couple who used to run it?"

"They've retired, I think. Moved out of the city."

"I always meant to go there," I say. "I can't believe I never got the chance."

Mom laughs. "Honey, you had twenty-nine years to go there. It's not like you missed out on something fantastic. Your dad and I went once. The only display was stick figures made of driftwood."

"Still," I say, sounding like a child and hating it. "A heads-up would have been nice."

I turn my gaze to the houses we pass. They're familiar. Brick and wood, and all of them with snow-heavy roofs. No place on Earth gets the snow Fairhill does. Even in Chicago, it doesn't stick. Not like it does here, in droves and piles and flurries, like a giant white blanket that refuses to lift for months.

We drive past the snowy football field. It's empty. "Mom, where's the Christmas Fair? It's gone!"

"They moved it," she says.

"They did?"

"Don't worry, it's still in town. It's at the high school football field now."

"But why? It's always been here. We could walk to it!"

"I think the city felt it took up too much space," she says. "Besides, the high school has needed better facilities."

"Too much space," I mutter. Perhaps I sound like a grumpy old man, but Fairhill isn't supposed to change.

It's not allowed to.

"While we're discussing changes, honey, I have something to tell you," she says, shooting me a hesitant smile. "We can't have a Christmas tree this year."

It's too much. *"No Christmas Tree?"*

"I know, sweetie. But it'll be okay."

"But why?"

"Evan called a few days ago. Sarah has a rare pine allergy."

I shake my head and shift deeper into my seat. At least the car seat warmer is as delicious as always. "Crap."

2

"Yes, it's a shame. But we can't make her feel bad about it. I love that she's finally joining us for the holidays."

"I agree," I say. We've spent little time with my brother's fiancée. "But still... a Christmas without a tree?"

"We'll survive. Oh, and you'll like this." Her voice rises an octave. "This is good news. Remember the house opposite ours?"

"The Dunbars'."

"Yes," she says. We still call it that, despite it being over a decade since the Dunbars moved. That family had imploded with scandal and drama. My brother's best friend had moved away, and he'd never returned.

"So? What about it?" I ask. Mom's employing dramatic pauses and I'm not in the mood.

"It's been sold," she says.

"Sold?"

"Yes. The family of four moved away. Guess who bought it?"

"The city," I say. "What, are they turning it into a gas station?"

Mom chuckles. "No. Adam bought it back."

"Adam. As in, Adam Dunbar?"

"Yes!"

I stare at her. For a long moment, I can't think of a single thing to say. "Why on Earth would he buy his parents' old house?"

"I don't know. Your dad speculates he bought it as an investment, but I think it's nostalgia. We asked why and he didn't really give us an answer. He works out of Chicago, you know." She turns to me with a half-smile. "Same as you, Holly."

"I know," I say, because I sure do. Adam Dunbar is my city's success story. The nerdy boy who'd survived his father's embezzlement scandal and their house being seized by creditors. The teenager who left Fairhill for an Ivy League college and founded a tech company.

The boy wonder.

3

The homegrown billionaire.

Once he'd been my brother's best friend, who I'd watched play basketball from the sidelines as sweat dampened his dark hair and the long lines of his body twisted in motion. He'd worn glasses. Then one summer he'd shot up in height and I'd realized he was the cutest boy in town. The crush had been as intense as it was one-sided.

"He's living there now," Mom continues. "Seems awfully lonely, though. It's a big house for one person."

"It's ludicrous," I say. "What is he doing? Recreating old memories?"

"Maybe. I told him to come over if he needed anything, but he hasn't. Your dad thinks Adam has help for that sort of thing, but I think he's just unsure. He's been gone from Fairhill a long time, you know."

"I know." I look down at my hands, covered by a pair of giant gloves. "Does Evan know Adam is back?"

"I texted him about it."

"And?"

Mom snorts. "He wrote back 'cool.' Sometimes I don't understand your brother, Holly."

"Sometimes I don't either."

"You always answer in complete sentences," she says, full of maternal pride. But then she takes a stab. "When you deign to text back."

I groan. "Mom, sometimes I'm at work, or I'm out with friends. I always reply, just not right away."

"I know, I know. You have a very important life down there. I just worry, honey. You're working too hard for a job that pays you too little."

I rest my head against the seat and close my eyes. "Mom, please. That's the way it is nowadays."

"I know and I won't nag. You've just gotten home. Just think about it, okay? There's more to life than work, and all that staring at the computer is going to ruin your eyesight. Remember what happened to your uncle."

"Jarrod wore the wrong prescription glasses for five years."

"And doesn't he regret it now." She pulls up on our street, and the familiar sense of home overtakes me. I could recite the order of mailboxes on Maple Lane from memory. Black, blue, white, white again, and then the red one I've opened thousands of times. Home. A wide driveway, a garage, and the two-story house I know every nook and cranny of.

I step out into the crisp Michigan air. Nothing is as beautiful as this street in the evenings with all the Christmas lights on.

I look at the Dunbars' house. The windows are dark, except in the living room. Light spills out behind drawn curtains.

"Oh, he's home," Mom says. She steps past me to the trunk and I help her with my bag. It's heavy. "Christ, honey."

"I'm actually moving home for good," I say, and it only feels like half of a joke. "There are a lot of Christmas presents in there."

"Oh, you shouldn't have," she says. "You have to save money."

"On Christmas? You know I have to win Secret Santa." Gift-giving is the best part of my favorite holiday, and I'm an expert. My theme of wrapping paper this year will win hearts across the nation.

"Not so fast, honey. I've put a lot of thought into mine."

I drag my giant suitcase toward the door, the wheels no good on the snowy path. I give the street one last glance. The living-room curtain in the Dunbars' house moves back into place and I catch the flash of a hand. Had Adam seen me come home?

Would he even remember Evan's little sister?

He'd spent most of his time with computers, even back then. Had been awkward at parties and hated his father's reputation. Mr. Dunbar had been Mr. Christmas himself, founder and CEO of the largest Christmas store in the state. Before the police came and the whole thing ended with him booking a one-way ticket out of the country. Adam had left Fairhill shortly after and never returned. My crush had withered away, but I'd never stopped looking out for him in the news and the papers.

Having Adam Dunbar living across the street is going to make Christmas a lot less relaxing…

…and a lot more interesting.

⚜

"Come on, boy. You can do it."

Winston pants at my side. He shouldn't, because it's cold out and we've barely made it around the block. But he is. And I refuse to accept it.

"You're doing great," I tell him. "You're such a good boy."

He trots along by my side, ears perked up at my voice, and keeps panting like he's run a marathon.

There had been a time when he'd raced next to my bike or gone running with me. Sure, that was over a decade ago, but it feels like yesterday.

It doesn't look like it feels like yesterday to Winston.

"You can do it. You know, exercise is food for our minds."

Winston looks up at me. Dark eyes that are annoyed, but steadfast. As steadfast as they've always been. His moustache makes him look dignified. Schnauzers can live up to sixteen and beyond.

"That's it," I say. "We're almost home, and then we can start a fire, and you can lie in front of it like the best boy in the whole world. I promise to give you a belly rub. Just never die, okay? How about you promise me you'll never, ever die? I'll feed you a steady diet of my shoes if you do."

Winston keeps shuffling along, neither confirming nor denying.

"I'll take your silence as a yes," I say. "Which means you can't break your word, bud."

A deep voice cuts through my one-sided conversation. "Do you always talk to him like he's on his deathbed? I'd find that very patronizing if I was him."

I stop dead. Winston immediately sits down on the cold side-walk, panting hard.

Adam Dunbar is standing in his driveway, leaning against a shovel. It's been over thirteen years since I saw him last.

It shows.

He's taller than I remember, towering over Winston and me. The skinny boy I'd had a crush on is gone. Adam has filled out, his parka stretching over wide shoulders. The glasses are gone too and dark hair falls unhindered over his forehead.

"Oh," I breathe. "Hi."

"Hello, Holly Michaelson." Dark eyes flash down to my still-panting dog. "And hello, Winston."

His curled tail wags.

"You're back in town," I say. Not to mention on his driveway at seven thirty a.m., which I hadn't expected when I threw on my sweatpants and put my hair up in a bun. On a scale of one to ten, I'm a solid minus two right now.

"Yes," he says.

"In your old house, too. Um… are you just visiting?"

A smile cuts through his dark beard. "Your parents have filled you in. Haven't they?"

"Yes. Sorry. It felt rude to assume, but yes, they told me you bought the house. Welcome back."

"Thanks," he says. His voice is deeper than I remember. "Although I should be the one saying that to you. Home for the holidays?"

"Yes. I realize Christmas is two weeks away, but I felt tired of the city. Besides, you know how Fairhill gets at Christmas. There's no place I'd rather be."

Adam looks down at Winston, his lips thinning. "Yes. Well, we've been overrun by visitors since the fair opened."

People drive to Fairhill from all around the state for our famous Christmas Fair, but even so, *overrun* seems a bit strong. "I like the fair," I say. "I've been craving one of the nutmeg hot chocolates since July."

"Sugar in a cup," he says.

I bend down to pet Winston, hiding my face from view. So he

doesn't like Christmas. Or sugar. The Adam I remember didn't like much either. "Yes," I mumble. "Well, I like them."

Our interactions had always been limited, even back then. We'd never really spent time together just the two of us. What do I say?

He clears his throat. "Your mother said you work in Chicago."

"I do," I say. "God, she hasn't talked your ear off about Evan and me, has she? She loves to talk about what we do and what we work with."

Another brief flash of his smile. "She hasn't."

"Good. I'm sure you're very busy these days. I mean, not busy enough to shovel your own driveway, clearly. But that's good. Good to spend some time outdoors. I'm keeping you from it, aren't I?"

I'm also rambling.

His eyes are steady. "You've grown up, Holly."

"Well, yes. I was a teenager last time I saw you."

"Yes. We all were." He looks across the road to my house. "Is Evan coming back for the holidays?"

"Yes. Everyone is, I think. A lot of people will be happy to see you." But even as I say it, I wonder if it's true. The citizens of Fairhill often speak about the Dunbars like a myth or a legend. Some with anger over Adam's dad, others with awe for Adam's work.

"Hmm," he says. "Well, take care, Holly. It was nice to see you again."

"Yeah, you too. Um, I don't always talk to Winston that way. I want you to know that."

He lifts up the shovel in a two-handed grip. "Just when you want him to do what you want."

"I suppose so, yes. That makes me sound awful, doesn't it?"

"It makes you sound human," he says. He nods to Winston, and it's as clear a dismissal as any. "I'd do as she says, if I were you."

I give him a wave as we trudge across the street. Winston huffs at my side. I feel the same way, and beneath my unwashed sweater and Dad's giant parka, my heart is pounding fast.

Adam Dunbar is back... and so is my stupid, unrequited crush.

2 Holly

I sit cross-legged on my twin bed, my laptop on my knees and pillows propped up behind me. It's the same story every time I go back home.

The bed is uncomfortable for the first two days before my body remembers, and then it's like I'm sixteen again, and it's the only one I've ever known.

"Honey!" Mom calls up the stairs. "Your father is going to stream something again. The wi-fi might slow down!"

"It won't. It hasn't for years!"

"Just wanted to give you a heads-up!"

I chuckle and reach over to rub Winston's floppy ear. He lets out a soft sigh and his tail starts to wag against my comforter. Our internet could handle ten teenagers playing World of Warcraft in high definition, but my mom remembers the time when Evan and I had fought over who had the right to be online.

I rub the spot between Winston's eyebrows. It's his favorite. "Besides," I tell him, "I'm just doing some light work."

That's a lie. I'm not writing the article on Gen Z fashion I should be for my "news" outlet. I'm researching tech billionaires.

Billionaire, really.

Adam Dunbar stares back at me from the screen. He's standing on a stage, dressed in simple black suit pants and a pressed white shirt. A tiny mic is attached to his shirt collar and his gaze is focused on the crowd. Even the title of the article is impressive. *Dunbar's ideas dazzle at 2018 Singapore Conference for Political Digitalization.*

His beard is much neater than it had been yesterday morning, cut to a close stubble. His dark hair is shorter too and rises neatly above his tanned face. He's aged into his features.

I flip through several other articles. One mentions how his company's decision to prohibit all talk of politics at the workplace had led to a better work environment. Several other tech giants had followed suit, leading to more productive break rooms and less contentious lunch meetings.

It's also very Adam, I think. Focused on the bottom line. Efficient.

For every article I read, it feels more and more bizarre that I met him two days ago across the street from my childhood home. Had an actual conversation, albeit brief.

"You were spoken to by an actual, real-life legend," I tell Winston. "He even stuck up for you. But you couldn't care less."

Winston illustrates my point by not moving an inch, his snout tucked between his front paws.

Chicago wunderkind sells half his shares in Wireout in one of the highest valuations of a tech company in over a decade. The sale puts the estimated value of Wireout at $42 billion.

My eyes read the sentence once, then twice. I turn to look out my window at the ordinary two-story house across the road. It's made out of brick. It has a beautiful porch and I remember Evan once saying it had a great basement.

But it's nothing for a man with that kind of money.

The man Fairhill never expected back. I might have known him once, but every single one of these articles makes it very clear that I don't anymore.

Sugar in a cup, he'd said yesterday about the Fairhill hot chocolates. The comment had played in my head several times. Did he mean to imply something? That I shouldn't be drinking them, or that I should think about my weight?

I shake my head. My ex-boyfriend had made comments like that. And sure, I've gained some weight over the past year. I'm not twenty-two and riding the high of a delayed growth spurt and college sports. But I like myself.

More and more, ever since my ex left my life.

Even if it's another area of my life where I've stalled. I used to be passionate about so many things, and now I'm working on articles about Bikram yoga and "what does his choice of emoji say about his personality?" for a website that's becoming more obsolete by the day. I'm almost thirty, and my journalistic dreams have nothing to show for them.

I look across the street again. His house is dark, the only one on the street without Christmas decorations or lights.

Adam Dunbar is just four years older than me.

"I'll catch up," I say, and then laugh. Because of course I won't. In four years I'll still be renting an apartment because I can't afford to buy and dating a string of men who talk to their mothers a little too often.

My phone buzzes.

Evan: I just looked at the game schedule you sent me for Christmas. Great job. But we need more charades. I'll figure something out.

I frown and text my brother back.

Holly: I've already planned a Christmas-themed charade session. We can do it with the cousins on the 26th.

He sends a Santa emoji.

Evan: Yes, but Sarah isn't very comfortable with charades. I think we should add one for Christmas Day just for the family. Something simple to warm her up. I'll fix it.

Holly: Okay. Good idea.

Sarah again. She's lovely, but she's my brother's fiancée and not mine. The thought makes me feel guilty and I toss my phone away. Our Christmas traditions are changing too. Subtly, perhaps, but they are.

The front door opens below and I hear the familiar voices of the ladies living on our street. A bunch of "hi"s and "hello"s and "how are you"s, the rustling of jackets being removed.

Mom is hosting a meeting with the Maple Lane Book Club.

I'd forgotten about that tradition, and I tiptoe to close my bedroom door.

But a voice below stops me. "Can you *believe* he still hasn't put up any lights?"

"No," another voice says. "Evelyn spoke to him just two days ago. He said no again. Gave absolutely no reason for it. Can you believe it?"

"Well," my mother says. "He might feel it would take too much time."

"Too much time? With his money, he could have someone do it for him. It ruins the street to have one house without Christmas lights. Jane, you know as well as I do that all those people will be coming to Fairhill for the Christmas Fair, and many of them will drive by here just to see our decorations. Maple Lane is famous!"

"I know, Martha," Mom says. She's wearing her patient voice.

"His refusal to hang a few simple lights will bring us all down!"

I grin at that. Martha sounds like we're one step away from the apocalypse, but that's her go-to mode. She'd been working up to an apoplectic fit when the garbage man was sick for a week.

"Can't you talk to him, Jane?" the soft voice says. "You know him well, don't you? Your boy was always spending time with the Dunbars, before they left."

Mom sighs. "That was a long time ago. I can ask, but if he's already said no to Evelyn... no, I have an idea. My daughter grew up with him too. They used to be friends. Holly! Holly, are you up there!"

I grip the doorpost. *Please don't.*

The stair creaks as she puts a foot on it. "Holly! Are you in a meeting?"

"No! I'm coming!"

Fifteen minutes and three encouraging pats on the back later and I'm pulling on my winter boots. I feel spectacularly unqualified to convince a billionaire business owner to please buy some Christmas lights for his house.

I look at the mirror in the hallway. At least my hair isn't in a bun today. It falls blonde and straight around my face, and it is newly washed, because I'm a responsible adult. The coat of mascara helps, but it can't fully hide my tired eyes.

I push open the door and trudge across the packed snow. Adam's house looks as calm and empty as always. Only the bottom floor and one of the windows on the second story have curtains.

"It's just your neighbor," I murmur to myself.

I knock on his wreathless door.

There's no response. I look over my shoulder and instantly wish I hadn't. Six nosy ladies are crowded in our living-room window watching me.

An audience. Awesome.

I knock again and rock back on my heels. I'll give it three more seconds, and then I can go home and say I tried.

"Who's there?" a deep voice calls out.

"Holly!"

Adam opens the door. Sweat glistens across a wide chest and down a flat stomach. A smattering of dark hair is clustered on his chest, and below his navel it disappears in a single line into his shorts.

Abs, I think. He has abs.

"Holly," he says. I pull my eyes up to his face. Dark hair clings to his forehead and he wipes it back with a towel.

He has earbuds in.

"I'm sorry," I say. "I didn't mean to interrupt whatever you're doing."

He holds up a single finger. "Duncan, something's come up on my end. I'll call back in two minutes."

I step back, shaking my head. *Don't,* I mouth.

But he pulls out his earbuds. "Already done. Sorry about that."

"No, I'm the one who should apologize. You're... working?"

He runs the towel over his neck. The muscles in his shoulders ripple. "A meeting with my team."

"Oh." My eyes drop down again. How does he conduct his meetings?

"I was cycling at the same time. Might as well sweat if I'm forced to endure meetings."

"Right. Um, that's clever. Saves time."

"Yes. I wasn't expecting you."

"No, I'm sorry," I say. "God, I think I've apologized four times now. Someone who says they're sorry all the time is so much worse than someone who never does."

His smile is a slash of white through his dark beard and flushed skin. "You can say it one more time, and then never again."

"Okay. Sorry for apologizing so much."

"There we go," he says. "You look good, Holly. No Winston this time?"

"I left him at home. Wasn't sure he'd survive the hike across the street."

"Good move. There's a lot of ice out there."

I nod and try to ignore the wide expanse of chest on display. "Are you getting cold? I'm sorry, I'll make this short."

Adam takes a step back. "Come in and I'll pretend I didn't hear you apologize again."

"Damn. Thank you." I step into the hallway and he shuts the door behind me. I knot my gloved hands together and look around. Boxes line the far wall. There are no rugs, no curtains. Nothing at all apart from a giant TV and a two-seater couch.

"Still getting settled?"

He snorts. "No. Not sure if I'm going to settle at all."

"Oh. Well, you've got the essentials down. A TV, a couch, an exercise bike somewhere. What more could a guy want?"

"That's what I'm thinking too, even if I've been told it looks sad. My assistant critiques it every time we have a video meeting."

I shake my head. "You should use one of those green screen backgrounds."

"Would save me a lot of trouble." He flips the headphones over in his hand, eyes locked on mine. Adam Dunbar had never looked at me like that when I was a kid—like someone worth talking to. Ending his meetings for. "So?" he says. "You said you came here for something? If you need to borrow flour or sugar, I'm sorry to disappoint."

I give a nervous laugh. "No, thanks. Got all that. No, this is actually… God, it's pretty stupid. But I was sent here on a mission."

"A mission?"

"Yes. Now that I'm talking to you, I don't want to say it."

He leans against the wall and crosses his arms over his chest. It's not distracting at all. "This sounds interesting," he says. "Tell me."

I close my eyes. "My mother is hosting the Maple Lane Book Club today."

"Right. Not what I expected you to say."

"They're talking about Christmas lights."

He groans. The sound is a deep masculine rumble, and I'm happy my eyes are closed. No need to see his abs while he sounds like that.

"Not you too, Holly."

"I'm sorry," I say, and then immediately shake my head. "Damn it, now I said it again. Feel free to put up Christmas lights or don't. I really don't mind either way, but I do mind what my mother's friends say to her, so that's why I'm here."

Adam raises an eyebrow. "How can Christmas lights matter so much?"

"It's Maple Lane," I say with a shrug, "and it's Fairhill in

December. Have you forgotten how crazy this town gets about Christmas?"

"I must have." He looks across the hall, into the empty kitchen. "They've clearly sent the big guns this time."

"Sorry? Oh, by sending me?" I shake my head. "Trust me, I won't mention it again."

"I don't like Christmas," he says. "What's the point of lighting up my house like a damn Christmas tree? It's wasteful. Light pollution is a real problem too, you know."

"Um, yeah. You're right about that," I say.

There had been a time when this house had been lit up like a skyscraper all of December, when Adam's father was Mr. Christmas. The house had been an advertisement for his store and all his new merchandise.

Adam sighs. "But they'd have me do it just so I won't ruin the look of the street. It's stupid."

"Well, that's a small town for you. Comes with the territory when you buy a house here."

Dark eyes return to mine, narrowing in thought. "Give it to me straight. Will I turn the town against me if I don't give in?"

"Well, Adam, I don't think Fairhill could ever turn against you. People here are so proud of you. You only lived here for a decade, but you're their greatest export. Do you remember the hairdresser on Main Street? Dave?"

"Vaguely."

"He has a sign in the window that says he used to cut Adam Dunbar's hair."

Adam stares at me. "He does?"

"Yes. Point being, it'll take a lot more than Christmas lights to turn people against you. But…"

"There's a but?"

"Yes. You are successful, and you've returned to a place where people like you never come to visit. We're not in Chicago or New York or LA at the moment. If you refuse to put up Christmas lights, you might come off as… well."

"Say it."

"Stuck-up," I say. "Too good for Maple Lane and Fairhill. People are already speculating about why you bought this place in the first place."

Adam takes a deep breath and my eyes drop to his expanding chest. He runs a hand through his hair. "Fine. I'll put up some lights. I'm guessing two spotlights won't do?"

I chuckle. "No, not really. There's a place outside of town that sells lights, cables, Christmas decorations. You should be able to get a lot of it there."

"Fine. I can't believe I'm giving in, by the way. I don't think I owe the town that after how it treated my mom and me. My father traded in Christmas shit, not me."

"I know," I say. "For what it's worth, I don't think you should do it if you don't want to."

He looks at me for a long moment. "Right. But if I don't, I'll be ostracized. Wait here."

He walks through the half-empty living room and disappears into the back, out of view. Muscles ripple over his back and I look down at my gloves. There's a hole right beneath the knuckle of my right index finger. I've had them for years. Every winter season, I say I'll buy a new pair. And every winter I don't get around to it.

Adam, on the other hand, works out while he handles business meetings.

"Holly," he calls. "Your mother told me you're a journalist?"

Oh, Lord. I clear my throat. "Yes. I went to journalism school."

"Where do you work?"

"It's an online publication. A website. We're not big, really."

He returns with a pen and notepad in hand. "Can you take the afternoon off?"

"Yes. Yeah. I'm writing a piece right now, but I can postpone it."

Happy to. I'd postpone it forever if I could.

Adam opens a thick wad of paper and scribbles on it. He pulls a piece out and hands it to me.

It's a check.

"What's this?"

"You accomplished your mission," he says. "I'll light up my house like a damn light bulb if the Maple Lane Book Club wants it. But I want you to pick out the lights."

I stare at the check and the obscene amount of zeroes. "You want me to buy all the decorations."

"You love Christmas," he says. "You said so just the other day."

"Yes, but…"

"And you could take the afternoon off."

"I did say that, didn't I?"

Another flash of his white smile and my heart stutters in my chest. He had been a cute seventeen-year-old, wicked smart and socially awkward, gangly and tall and witty.

It's not fair that he grew into his looks like this. It's devastating.

"Please," he says. "I'll owe you one, Holly. Come back later and I'll hang them with you. We can order food too. For old time's sake."

I look down at the check. "You might regret this."

"Make me," he says.

3 Adam

I'm smiling as I get back on the exercise bike. Holly Michaelson, Evan's little sister, is all grown up. And she's cute.

She'd been cute back then too, but not in a way I'd really seen. She'd been younger than us. Not an option. Not like now. Not like… no. Evan and I might not have spoken in over a decade, but she's still his little sister.

But she'd snuck a peek at my chest. I'd seen it.

"Adam?"

"Yup," I tell my assistant. Duncan's connected to my headphones, sitting miles and miles away. "I'm back."

"This is about February's schedule."

"I know. Continue."

But as he runs through the appointments and offers for next year, and I start pedaling again, my mind goes back to Holly.

I didn't think she'd say yes. Had been a hundred percent sure she'd hand me back the check. I don't know what compelled me to give it to her. To see if she would accept, perhaps. Up the ante. Challenge her like she was challenging me. And maybe, just maybe, I wanted an excuse to spend time with her.

I finish up my meetings and take a shower. I've just put on clothes when the door rings. "Coming!"

Holly is standing outside. She's in a too-large winter coat, blonde hair tucked beneath a beige hat. Her arms are filled with boxes.

"You're going to regret this," she tells me.

I open the door wide. "Come in," I say. "Is that a reindeer on the box?"

"Yes. You gave me carte blanche with that check, you know."

"I'm aware." I look out the door toward her car. "How much more is there?"

"Oh, the trunk is full."

"Holly," I groan. Her name feels sweet on my tongue.

She puts down the packages in the hallway. I pull on my boots and head out toward the car. Two rounds later and all of her purchases are in my hallway, right next to the moving boxes.

"You went all out," I say. The boxes have disgustingly cheerful illustrations on them. Christmas trees and Santas and smiling, happy families. All fooled into thinking commercialism is the key to happiness.

"Yes. Maybe I shouldn't have. But," Holly says, turning to me with an admonishing glint to her eyes, "you sent me out to do your errands."

"I think you needed a break. Tell me you didn't enjoy spending that outrageous amount on Christmas decorations."

She pauses with her back to me, eyes on the packages. "Okay, all right. I enjoyed it. I think I love Christmas as much as you hate it."

"Then you must love it very much indeed," I say. Blonde hair has escaped from her braid, curling in wispy tendrils at her neck. Her sweater is huge and red and fuzzy. It's cute. All of her is cute, just like she'd been at fourteen, Evan's sister who blushed whenever I spoke to her.

But she's not blushing now.

"So?" she asks, turning to look at me. "Shall we?"

The next hour is a study in patience for me. There are cables and cables and cables, and I quickly discover that while Holly has a creative eye, she's not good at electrics.

"I should get a switchboard," I mutter from the hallway. "There's no way to easily unplug all of this at the end of the night."

"Do you have to?"

"Yes. Think of the electricity bill. Of the light pollution."

She's standing on a ladder she dug out of her father's garage, hanging string lights along the second-floor balcony. There's a smile in her voice. "God, yes. The light pollution!"

"It's a serious problem."

"Right." She's reaching up high and despite her puffer jacket, a sliver of skin is visible above the edge of her jeans. "Hand me the roll of fairy lights?"

I lift it up to her. My hands are getting stiff from the cold. "Thank you," I say. "But you'll have to tell me if I'm keeping you from something important. For all I know, you might be hard at work against a deadline. What newspaper are you with?"

She snorts. "I think calling it a newspaper is a bit generous."

"Oh? Wait, we need to move the ladder. Come on, come down."

Holly slides down and lands with a soft crunch in the snow. The top of her head, including the tassel on her hat, reaches to my chin. I move the ladder for her and hold it steady.

"So?" I ask. "Your newspaper isn't really a newspaper?"

She climbs up. "No. It's an online publication."

"An online publication," I repeat.

"It's a website, really. I write and research blog posts."

"Oh."

"But don't worry. A few more posts about pimple popping and astrology, and I'll be right in line for the Pulitzer. More lights?"

"There's not much left."

She tacks the end of it to the house, right above the bottom floor windows. "Maybe I should have gotten more."

"No."

Holly laughs. "Right. Of course not. But don't worry, Mr. Scrooge, because I have things for your front lawn as well."

"I saw that."

"You sound so excited." She climbs down the ladder and lands in front of me with a wide smile. "I bought a family of reindeer."

"Uh-huh."

"Including a little baby fawn."

I groan, and she laughs again. "It'll be cute. Come on, let's unbox them."

I follow her into my box-strewn hallway. "Stupid reindeer."

"Wasn't a reindeer the logo of your dad's store?" she asks without looking at me, bending at the waist to lift up the fawn. I watch her for a moment.

"Yes," I say.

But the last thing I want to talk about is my father and his Christmas store. The one thing he spent his entire year working toward, and when the holidays came, the reason he was never home. He made a killing from poor saps who thought Christmas wasn't Christmas without glossy wrapping paper and inflatable Santas on their roofs.

Holly walks past me. "Adam?"

"Yeah. Coming." I lift up the large reindeer and muscle it out the door after her. A quick glance around Maple Lane shows it as quiet as usual. No one here to witness my shame.

Holly is effective and likes to talk. I listen to her happy, nerve-tinged chatter as we set up the animal family on my front lawn. They're plastic and metal and lights, and they look completely lifeless.

"There we go!" she says. "This will look great lit."

"I'll take your word for it." I tug at the collar of my shirt. "It's freezing outside. Come on, let's get inside. I promised you food."

She gives me a slanted half-smile. "Right. Yes, you did."

"Can't let Evan's little sister starve."

I close the front door after her and tug off my jacket. I'm halfway into the kitchen when I realize she hasn't started taking off hers yet. She's standing in the hallway, hands clasped.

"Holly?"

"Yeah. Look, you don't have to have me over for dinner, you know. If that was just something you said to be polite earlier. I'm sure you're crazy busy."

I shake my head. "Don't be silly. Come in. Do you like Chinese?"

She nods and starts to slowly unlace her giant snow boots. "Yes."

"Good. There's a place here that does home delivery."

"The one place in Fairhill," she says. "Dennis will drive out the food to us."

I grab the menu. "Yes. I'm probably his best customer."

She steps into the kitchen behind me. Snug, skinny jeans hug her legs beneath the giant red sweater. Her cheeks are flushed with the bite of cold. "Wow."

"Wow?"

"You really haven't settled in at all."

I look around my kitchen. It has the necessities, but it's no home. A brief pang of embarrassment rushes through me as I see it with her eyes. Little Holly Michaelson, who always had big dreams and the eyes of a romantic. "No. I suppose I haven't. "

She leans against the counter. "I'll have the Moo Shu pork."

I nod, glancing over the menu. "I'll get us some prawn crackers and a side of stir-fry too."

"Thanks."

"Least I can do," I say. "You probably saved me from the ladies of the Maple Lane Book Club descending on my front door with pitchforks."

Holly smiles, eyes locking on mine. "You don't strike me as someone who would mind."

"I don't? Well, then I suppose I wanted your company."

My words are bold. They hang in the air between us, an unexpected offering. I don't take it back. It's true.

She smiles. "Well, in that case, I want a Pepsi Max too."

"Coming right up."

Twenty minutes later, Dennis leaves with a handsome tip and I return to the kitchen with a white bag that smells like heaven. Holly is sitting cross-legged beside my couch. There's a newspaper in her hands.

Over the top of her head, I can see which page she's reading. *Damn.*

"Food's here," I say.

She turns, a smile lighting up her face. "The *Chicago Tribune* wrote a piece on you?"

"Seems like it, yes."

"How did you get it here?"

"My assistant sent it over." I unpack the food onto the counter. The piece she's reading isn't bad. It's been vetted and double-checked. But it's an odd thing to see that part of my life in her hands. The past touching the present.

Who I was and who I am colliding.

"Fairhill's golden child," she says. "Everyone here is so proud of you, you know? But I'm sure you know that."

"Didn't seem like it when I had to leave," I mutter.

Holly glances over. "Oh. I'm sorry."

I shake my head. "Doesn't matter. Come on, the food will get cold."

She puts the newspaper down and joins me by the kitchen table. The sleeves of her giant sweater cover half of her hands and she has to fold them up before eating.

"For what it's worth," she says, "I never wanted you and your family to leave. Before. When everything happened, I mean."

I look down at my mix of noodles. "Yeah. Thanks, Holly."

We eat in silence for a minute. She breaks the silence, voice aiming for cheery. "I read that you sold half of your company. How come?"

This, I know how to speak of. I explain IPOs and outside investment and the sense of being trapped, despite being the only one calling the shots. "Wireout has been my life for over a decade. I dropped out of college for it, you know. Now I want more freedom. A healthier relationship to it."

Holly props her head in her hand, her blue eyes thoughtful. "That makes sense to me."

"It does?"

She nods. "In the article I just read, you said you used to work ninety-hour weeks. I don't think that's healthy for anyone."

I shrug. "It was a must at the time."

"What are you down to now? Sixty?" Her eyes dance, a smile on her lips. "Fifty?"

"I plead the fifth. But it's a more reasonable amount, yes."

"Were you really working earlier? While you were... um." Her eyes drop to my chest.

My smile widens. "Yes. I often take meetings while I'm on the exercise bike. Why not?"

"Right. Well, I often write while I'm in my pajamas. Almost as impressive."

I picture Holly, hair loose and in a camisole, sitting in front of her computer. "Yes. Definitely."

"So you don't like Christmas," she says, looking down at her near-empty box. "Adam, why did you buy this house, then? You know how this city gets."

I groan. "A tactical error on my part."

"It's only going to get worse, you know. We have two weeks left until Christmas."

"I know."

"The Christmas Fair is in full swing. They're already bringing out the horse and carriage rides, my mom and I went to the Christmas tree lighting ceremony yesterday, there's the—"

"I know," I say. "I'll have to figure out a way to avoid it."

Holly's smile turns crooked. "It's the best time of the year."

"It's the most stressful, chaotic, commercialized time of the year."

"Oh, Adam. No."

I shrug again. "I'm not sorry."

"But it's the *best*, coziest, most heartwarming time."

Her eyes are earnest and teasing and warm as they lock on mine. Like she sees me, like she's not assessing me or considering her words carefully. There's no cautious planning in her gaze.

"You'll have to show me, then," I hear myself say.

"I can do that," she says.

"Friday night. Do you have plans?"

She shakes her head. "No."

"Christmas Fair, then. Let's see if you can change my mind."

4 Holly

"**I** think you prevented World War Three, honey." Mom is peering out of our kitchen window at the Dunbars' house, the red Christmas curtains pulled back. "I don't know how you got him to agree."

"I'm not sure anyone can get Adam to agree to anything he doesn't want to do," I say. "But I told him this was the easier path."

"Smart man," Dad calls from the living room. He has his feet up on the coffee table while Mom is in the other room. "No one wants to get on the wrong side of the Maple Lane Ladies!"

"We're not that bad," Mom protests.

"You're not," I say. "You can't say the same for some of the others. Martha is a shark."

Mom laughs and lets the curtain fall back into place. "Come on."

"I'm not wrong."

She doesn't comment. Her eyes look me over instead, stopping at my lips. I'm wearing a dark red shade. "Are you going somewhere?"

"Just out." I pass her in the kitchen and reach for a home-baked gingerbread cookie. "The Christmas Fair."

"Didn't you go with Fallon just earlier in the week?"

"Yes, but I'm going with Adam."

Mom makes a long *ooh* sound and I shake my head. "Don't."

"So that's why he agreed to put up the Christmas lights."

"Mom," I protest. "He's a gazillionaire who's for some reason decided to hide out in Fairhill for a few months. None of us know why he bought the old house, but we all know he's not going to stay. He's not *ours* anymore."

"We don't know that," she protests. "Maybe he'll settle here. Open up his dad's old store."

"That's the absolute last thing he's going to do."

Mom shrugs and flattens out the wrapping paper in front of her on the kitchen table. She's wrapping Christmas gifts for my cousin's new baby. "You're probably right about that. It sure didn't end well."

"That's an understatement," I murmur. The Dunbar Christmas Store had imploded. From being one of the state's largest, exporting goods all across the country, to the CEO and owner being charged with embezzlement and fraud.

Adam's dad had fled the country, and to the best of my knowledge, he hasn't returned. It had been the talk of the town. The creditors had seized their house.

From one day to the next, Adam and his mother stood on the street.

Mom hums "White Christmas" to herself as she places a box of Legos on the wrapping paper. I lean against the counter. "About that, actually. Did we help them?"

"Hmm?"

"Adam and his mother. After the Dunbar store collapsed."

She cuts through the paper in precise movements. "Well, they had family to stay with, honey. Adam went back to college right away and Evelyn went to live with her sister for a bit."

"Did you see her again?"

Mom looks up. "Once or twice, but we were never really friends, honey. Just neighborly. She kept herself apart."

I run a hand over my neck. "But we didn't… I don't know. Reach out? I remember a lot of people were really angry at Mr. Dunbar."

"Well, some people lost a lot of money. He mostly embezzled from company clients, but there were normal people in there. A few contractors who lost a season's worth of pay."

"Right. I remember that."

She starts to wrap the present. "But that was never Adam or his mother's fault, of course. It can't have been easy to live with him as a husband or a father."

"I don't remember him well," I say. Mr. Dunbar had always been busy, or in the background. Arriving for neighborhood barbeques only to disappear again on phone calls. Adam had been this lonely character, walking next to my brother, the two of them in glasses and their heads bent over a game or a book. He'd seemed apart, even then. Not quite of Fairhill.

"You didn't miss much," Mom says.

A car horn sounds outside. From behind the Christmas curtains I spy his giant Jeep parked outside our house. Nerves appear in my stomach, fluttering on gossamer-thin wings. I'm almost thirty. I've been on a ton of dates in my life, many bad, some good. And it's been over a decade since I had a crush on Adam Dunbar.

But my body doesn't seem to know any of that.

"Have fun, honey," Mom says. "Remember, your dad and I are leaving early tomorrow for your aunt and uncle's."

"And you'll be gone all weekend. I know," I say. "I'll take care of Winston."

"Thanks, honey."

"Keep an eye on the weather report!" Dad calls. "They're warning about a snowstorm coming in. It should pass north of us, but I've stacked some extra firewood indoors just in case."

"Okay, I will!"

"Bye!"

"Bye, see you later!"

I finally make it onto the slippery driveway. Adam is in the front seat of his giant Jeep, watching me Bambi my way out to his car. My breath makes a plume of white in the cold air.

I have to tug twice to get the passenger door open. Adam is wearing a crooked grin, watching me climb into his car. Thick hair falls over his forehead. "Hello."

My voice is breathless. "Hi."

"You kept me waiting."

"Sorry. Dad felt it was the right time to lecture me about watching the weather reports."

"An important pastime," Adam says. He puts the car in drive and the four-wheel rolls over the icy street like it's child's play. The seats smell like leather and money and a man who has his life together.

I think of my tiny little Honda, still in my too-expensive parking garage in the city. It's two months past its service date.

"So," Adam says. "Little Holly Michaelson is going to show me the Christmas Fair."

I groan. "Little," I say. "How demeaning. Is that how you used to think of me?"

"Well, you were little," he says. "Only fourteen when I left for college, right?"

"You remember?"

"I did the math yesterday." He turns away from Maple Lane, one hand on the steering wheel.

"You were always good at math," I say. It's a stupid comment, but he smiles. It's a quirk of his lips.

"You remember that," he says.

"Of course I do. You and Evan would do your homework at the kitchen table sometimes."

"I helped you once. With your calculus."

I nod and knot my hands together in my lap. "Yes. Thank you."

He laughs again. In this car, the sound envelops me. With every gesture I feel myself sinking deeper into my old crush. "I'm pretty sure you already said thank you for that, Holly. Fifteen years ago."

"Well, just in case," I say.

"Well, you're welcome," he says. "It was my pleasure."

Heat blooms in my chest and I focus on the road ahead. Keeping my gaze away from tempting half-smiles.

The street in front of the high school is lined with cars. "It might be pretty full," I say. Stating the obvious.

"Half of them are probably from out of town," he mutters.

I smile. "Spoken like a true Fairhillite. Are you becoming one of us again?"

"Never," he says, but he doesn't sound like he means it. Adam finds a spot opposite the entrance and parallel parks like a champion. I watch the smooth rotation of the wheel, the strong column of his neck as he looks over his shoulder.

It would have been so much easier if he hadn't grown up to be *this*. Still his old self, with charming half-smiles and intelligence, but with the added layer of so much competence and masculinity.

He catches me staring and a slow smile spreads across his face. "All good, Holly?"

"Yes," I say. "Just thinking about how much you'll hate the fair."

He groans. "Don't remind me. I'm doing this for you, you know."

"Oh, are you?"

"Yes."

"It's not because you bought a house in a town you have no friends in?" I say. It's meant as teasing, but I immediately regret it.

It must show on my face because Adam chuckles. "Harsh, but fair. I don't think fourteen-year-old you would have said that to me."

"She's horrified inside, I promise."

He smiles and nods out the window. "Shall we horrify her some more and go to the Christmas Fair together?"

"Yes," I say.

But she wouldn't be horrified by that, I think. *She'd be squealing in joy.*

The entrance is packed and we have to squeeze through the crowd to reach the ticket booth. Giant Christmas trees flank the entrance and Frank Sinatra croons from the speaker system.

"Oh," I breathe. "It's fantastic."

Adam snorts at my side. "Look at all their bags. It's a mall with a Christmas theme."

I nudge him. "They're Christmas gift shopping."

"Yes, because nothing says Christmas like parting with your hard-earned cash and buying things no one wants or needs."

"You're in a bad mood tonight."

He shakes his head and gives me a sage look. "With age comes wisdom, little Holly."

"You have to stop calling me that."

He buys us two tickets at the entrance booth. It isn't until we're inside that he answers me. "Do I?"

"I'm not little anymore. I have a job, a car, an apartment."

"In Chicago." Adam steers me around a popcorn stall. The scent of buttery corn is delicious and mouth-watering and not nearly as interesting as this conversation. "I live there too, nowadays. When I'm not buying property in Fairhill."

"Which happens a lot."

He snorts. "Once, and I'm not keen to repeat it."

I bite my lip. I want to ask why he's back, why he bought that house, but something tells me he won't talk about it in the middle of Fairhill High and the giant Christmas Fair it hosts.

I grip his forearm. "Let me give you the full tour, then. All of my favorite places."

"God help me," he mutters. "Lead the way."

Despite his previous comment, I take him to Ginna's Hot Chocolate stall. The giant line should be proof enough that it's a necessity.

But I go on the offensive just in case. "Sure, it's a treat, but it's Christmas," I say. "It's also cold in here. No visit would be complete without it."

Adam looks over my head at the giant copper vat of hot chocolate brewing. "Uh-huh. As long as I get whipped cream on mine, I'm okay."

"Oh. Well, that can be arranged."

"I mean a lot, Michaelson. Copious amounts."

I grin up at him. "Who knew Adam Dunbar had such a sweet tooth?"

"Everyone who's ever done my grocery shopping for me," he

says. Then he frowns. "That sounded very out of touch with reality, didn't it?"

I laugh. "Yes. But I guess that's your reality, isn't it? Shiatsu massages after your workouts, personal assistants handling your email, monster cars that are serviced perfectly?"

"I have never once had a Shiatsu massage."

I cluck my tongue. "All that money and no sense. Massages are the best part of life."

"Oh yeah?"

"Yeah. If I were you I'd have one every single week."

"I think that would be hard to accomplish in Fairhill."

"When you get back to Chicago, then, and your fancy Christmas-hating lifestyle."

"My fancy lifestyle," he repeats. Adam shakes his head, eyes narrowing as he looks at me. "You're just the same, Holly. Like you were when we were kids."

"Just the same?"

"You never let Evan off the hook. It was like you were twins, without the age gap."

"My mom definitely thought that when we were small. I don't know if you lived here back then, but she dressed us in matching outfits."

Adam groans. "No."

"Yes. We have pictures of Evan and me as sailors, cowboys, and even astronauts once. I really hope that was for Halloween."

He laughs. "Astronauts. She had high hopes for your careers."

We shuffle forwards, the line moving slow. "Yes, but instead she got an insurance salesman and a failed journalist. Shoot for the stars and land on the moon, right?"

"You're not a failed journalist."

"No, no, you're right. I'm one of the greats. My piece on pimple popping changed lives."

"So you're in the beginning of your career. Lots of people are. That doesn't mean you're a failure. Would you call an Olympic athlete who's only halfway done with his training a failure?"

"You can't compare me to an Olympian!"

"Why not? Who knows what pieces you'll write in a decade?"

I shrug, my cheeks heating up. He's right, even if I'm getting a pep talk from someone who was a millionaire by age twenty-three, a wunderkind, a coding genius. But the last thing I want is for him to think I'm self-pitying.

"You're right," I say.

"Damn straight I am," he says. "But you don't sound convinced."

I look down at my boots. The leather is slightly scuffed at the toes, but they've seen me through six winters without a complaint. "I guess I'm just in a rut right now. But you're right. I hear you."

"That's right," he says, and a strong shoulder nudges mine. "Why don't you write an article about Fairhill? Shop it around to a few newspapers. This place is ripe for investigative journalism."

I smile. "So many seedy business dealings going on, you mean?"

"Oh yes. Weird characters lurking around every corner. Why would a grown person spend six months of the year painting ceramic Santas just to sell them at the Christmas Fair? Are they secretly stashed with drugs?"

I look over his shoulder, but the people behind us in line can't hear. So I rise up on my tiptoes and whisper in his ear. "Why does Ginny's hot chocolate really have such a long line? What does she put in the drink?"

His hand rests on the low of my back. It burns, even through my layers. "What about the Christmas light-obsessed mafia of Maple Lane? What are they really hiding?"

I put a hand over my mouth to stop the laughter that rocks through me. Adam's eyes spark with amusement, locked on mine. "Sounds like a killer article."

"Investigative journalism at its finest."

"Next!" Ginny calls out. The scent of cocoa hangs thick in the air.

"Hi Ginny," I say. "I'd love two hot chocolates, please. With lots and lots of whipped cream."

She smiles at us both, cheeks red from exertion and the cold. "Coming right up. Nice to see you, Holly. Wouldn't be Christmas without you back in town!"

"No, it wouldn't be Christmas without your hot chocolate." I hand her a bill and accept a steaming cup. Adam takes his with a murmured thank you.

Ginny nods at him. "Good to see you here, Dunbar."

"Thank you."

"Next!"

We stroll through the fair, past the tiny petting zoo and the stalls selling Christmas presents. He finally takes a sip of the hot chocolate.

"Admit it," I say. "It's absolutely fantastic."

Adam looks at me over the rim of his cup. "It's great. It tastes exactly like hot chocolate should."

"Right?"

"But that doesn't mean that all this," he says, sweeping his arm out at the crowds milling around us, "isn't an excuse for companies to make money."

"You're hopeless. Come on, I have one more ace up my sleeve."

I lead us past the stall with the potentially drug-stashed ceramic Santas, past someone selling gloves, past the hot-dog stand. Right to where all the kids and teenagers are clustering. "You can't say this is commercialized. This is just pure, unadulterated fun."

"Throwing hoops on reindeer antlers?" Adam asks.

"Yes. Or fishing for baubles. Take your pick, Dunbar. Just know I'm going to wipe the floor with you."

He raises an eyebrow. "I don't have to enjoy it to be excellent at this, Holly."

"You can't be excellent at everything. It's humanly impossible. I'll also have you know that I've trained for years."

"Hmm. I can imagine that, actually."

"Scared?"

"Never." He takes a deep sip of his hot chocolate and reaches inside his jacket for his wallet. "Let's see what you've got, little Holly."

I shake my head at him and he grins, unrepentant. Five minutes later and we're standing elbow to elbow, side by side, with plastic hoops in our hands. A bored teenager is manning the stall. He's watching something on his phone and not paying any attention to us.

Which is just as well, because this will be carnage. I won't lose.

"Come on, Rudolph," I mutter, twisting the ring in my hands. "Be on my side."

Adam snorts. "Are you praying to a fictional character?"

"He's right in front of us, buddy." I take aim and throw the hoop. It lands on one of the antler points and stays there, a red ring of victory. *"Yes!"*

"Just you wait." Adam throws three in quick succession. The first two go wide, with only the last ring managing to snag on an antler point. He curses in a very un-holiday-like manner.

I lean against his side. "Not as easy as you thought, huh?"

"All I need is practice."

"Right." I toss my remaining two and both score, looping around points of the plastic reindeer's antlers. I take a tiny bow in his direction. "Thank you, my Lord and Savior, oh Rudolph."

"You've done this way too often," Adam mutters.

"Oh, just every single winter."

"That's it. I want a re-match."

We play twice more. I win another round, but the final one is tied. It's more thanks to a bad throw from me than Adam's skill, but he treats it like a victory.

"Don't feel bad," he says. "That could have happened to anyone."

I poke him in the side. "Don't get cocky. I won that two-to-zero."

"We'll find something I'm good at. Have you ever coded? Created an app from scratch?"

"No, and that's not a Christmas Fair game," I say. "But this one is. Have you ever bobbed for baubles?"

Adam stares at the giant tub of floating baubles. "I remember this one, but only faintly. Please tell me we don't have to stick our faces in."

"We'll use a fishing rod. It's like hook-a-duck, but the Christmas edition."

"Right. Because we're freezing while we do it."

I chuckle. "You're a ball of sunshine."

"And you're brave," Adam says. "Fishing is my sport, you could say."

"Really?"

"No."

I nudge him again, giddiness like a cloud inside me. I feel like I'm floating. "Stop it."

"But I'm a quick learner. Let's go, Michaelson. Winner takes the glory."

He hooks three baubles in the same time it takes me to hook one. My cold fingers are stiff around the fishing rod, and despite my intense focus, the baubles slip away.

Adam looks pleased with himself when the timer rings. I give him a skeptical look. "Not a fisherman, huh?"

He shrugs. "If fishing was as easy as picking baubles out of a kiddie pool, I'd be the state champion."

"Maybe this is for the best. You won one, I won one. We're on even footing."

"We are," he says. "You know, I thought tonight would be the worst. But so far it's been okay."

I press a hand to my chest. "Wow, what a compliment. I'm swooning."

His smile turns into a chuckle. "Yeah, that wasn't the best phrasing, was it?"

"Not really. Is that how you sweep women off their feet back in Chicago?"

"By telling them I find it tolerable to spend time with them? No." His hand returns to my low back, walking closer than necessary. "Are you in any position to be swept off your feet, then?"

Nerves make it hard to speak. "I'm not already swept by someone, no. You know how I said I was in a bit of a rut? That applies to my love life too."

"What a shame," he says. He doesn't sound like he means it.

"Yes. Very sad indeed. So I'm drowning myself in holiday cheer instead."

"That's one thing the holidays are good for," he says. "They take people's mind off things."

"Are you saying something good about Christmas?"

He grimaces. "It's a statement, not a compliment."

"I won't tell anyone."

"Good."

I smile up at him, and he looks down at me, dark eyes bottomless. They make it hard to hold on to my train of thought. I wish we could stay here forever, laughing about nothing at all.

His lips quirk. "Did you say you had Christmas shopping left to do?"

"Oh! That's right! I have to get something for our Secret Santa game."

"I'll come with you."

I walk us through stalls, nodding hello to a few people as we go. If Adam notices the curious looks shot his way, he doesn't let it show. There are plenty of people here who have no clue who he is… but the locals do.

I don't know if they're looking at him because he's Adam Dunbar, the genius behind Wireout and one of the youngest self-made billionaires in America, or if it's because he's Adam Dunbar of the infamous Dunbar Christmas Store.

Probably both.

We come to a stop in front of a tiny stall where Josh Perkins sells handmade snow globes. Inside are carved replicas of Fairhill, complete with Main Street, the Christmas Fair in its new place, and the town's Christmas tree in the center. Josh spends months on these.

"Hi there, Holly." He inclines his head to Adam. "Who's your fella?"

"This is Adam," I say. "We're doing some last-minute Christmas shopping."

"You have almost two weeks left, so not that last minute," he says. "You should see the lines here on Christmas Eve!"

"Gosh, I can imagine."

"Looking for anything in particular?"

I point at a medium-sized snow globe with Fairhill in the center. It's on a beautiful white base, complete with painted snowflakes. "I'd like to buy that one, please."

"Coming right up. Gift-wrapped?"

"No, thank you. I'll do that at home."

"Just as well," Josh says. "These hands are good for making, not for prettying."

"I don't know about that," I say. "The snow globes are plenty pretty."

He gives a half-grunted agreement and starts wrapping the snow globe in tissue paper.

Beside me, Adam bends his head. "You're actually buying a snow globe?" he murmurs.

"Yes," I whisper.

"I can't believe it."

I nudge him with my elbow to stay silent. He does, but it's not for long. We've barely made it three feet away before he shakes his head. "I appreciate you wanting to support local businesses, but a snow globe? What are you going to do with that?"

"Stare at it wistfully eleven months of the year," I say.

Adam shakes his head. "I don't get your obsession with this holiday."

"I don't get your hate for it," I say. "But it's not for me, actually. It's for Evan's fiancée. I got her for our family Secret Santa."

"Secret Santa," he repeats.

"Yes. We do it every year, but this is the first time Sarah's joining. I want to make her a box of everything that makes Fairhill Fairhill. Introduce her to Evan's past and the family, you know? I have a few pictures from Evan's yearbook in there and his favorite recipes, the ones Mom always makes. I wrote a guide to Fairhill. I even got the calendar Fairhill's fire department made for next year. Evan's going to love having half-dressed firemen at home if Sarah hangs it up. And now I have this snow globe!"

Adam's eyes are impossible to read and he says nothing. I grip my box with the snow globe tighter. "Does it sound silly?"

"No. It sounds… very you."

"I'm not sure if that's a compliment."

"It is," he says. "Trust me."

My throat feels dry. "Thank you."

"Do you like Sarah?"

"Evan's fiancée?"

"Yes."

"I do. She's nice. She's… exactly what he needs, I think. It'll be fun to have her over for Christmas."

Adam raises an eyebrow. "You don't sound convinced."

"No, no, I am. It'll be really nice. It's just, it'll change the vibe, I suppose. She's allergic to pine so we're skipping the Christmas tree this year, and we never have before." I shrug. "It's silly. It's a small thing, but I miss it."

He nods. "I understand."

"Despite Christmas trees being commercialized nonsense?"

"Yes," he says. "Despite that."

That makes me smile. "You're hopeless. What are your plans for Christmas, Mr. Scrooge?"

"Not much," he says. He turns toward the center stage. The high school band has started playing again, the tune of a wonky "All I Want for Christmas" belting out across the fair.

"Will you be here? In town?"

"I haven't decided yet."

"Okay," I say. I still don't quite know what happened to his parents after everything, and there's no easy way to ask. "Let me know if you are, so I know if I should get you your own snow globe."

He groans. "Holly, don't you dare."

"I saw the way you were staring at the ones back there. There was lust in your eyes. Pure, unadulterated desire."

"Lust," he repeats, looking down at me. "No, there certainly wasn't."

"Yes," I murmur. "You want to celebrate Christmas, deep down."

"No," he says, just as quietly. "I really don't."

My throat feels dry. His eyes are dark brown and steady and I want to get to know him. Everything about him is interesting to me. Adam Dunbar, the enigma I never got to solve.

Maybe he'll let me this time around.

"Hey, are you Dunbar?" a man's voice asks. He's standing in front of us in a jacket with reflexive tags, eyes narrowed. "Adam Dunbar?"

Adam meets the middle-aged man's gaze with a cool one of his own. "I am, yes."

"Lenny Mauritz," he says and extends a hand. Adam shakes it. "I worked for your father back in the day. He hired my uncle's construction company for that expansion, down on Turrell Street?"

"I know which one you mean," Adam says. His voice isn't unkind, but it's cold. Like he knows what's coming.

Dread drops in my stomach. *Please don't, Lenny.*

But Lenny does.

"Well, your old man screwed us over good. An entire year's worth of income, lost, and we haven't seen a single penny of it. My uncle had to sell the house to balance the books that year." Lenny's voice rises, anger seeping into it. "You don't know where he is, do you? I'd love to tell him just what people here think of him."

"I don't know where he is," Adam says.

"You sure? Last I heard, he wasn't in the country. Fleeing from justice. But would he really leave his only kid in the dark? I doubt it."

His tone is bothering me. "Adam's not responsible for what his father did," I say.

Lenny looks at me, like he's surprised there's someone else here. "'Course not," he says. "But he might help make them right. None of what Dunbar did was right. Your father's an asshole, and I'm not afraid to say it."

"Clearly not," Adam mutters. He reaches for the inside pocket of his jacket and pulls out his wallet. "How much did your uncle's company lose in expected income? What does my father owe them?"

"Enough to keep his company going for a year," Lenny says. He eyes Adam's wallet with suspicion. "Even you can't carry that much cash around."

"I don't," Adam says. He extends his business card. "Contact me on that email address with the full list of what you and your uncle are owed in voided contracts. I'll make sure you get paid."

Lenny stares at the business card in Adam's hand. "It's a little too late, isn't it? Your father should have done that years ago, the bastard. Instead he's lying on some beach with a drink and all of our money."

Adam's voice is clipped. "Well, this is the best you're going to get. Take it or leave it."

Lenny accepts the business card. "Right."

"I'm sorry about what happened in the past," Adam says. "But I can't do anything more than this, I'm afraid. I don't know where he is."

"Thank you," Lenny says. The words sound reluctant. "I'll be in touch, you know. With the full amount. For my uncle and his employees too."

"Please do."

Lenny nods at us both. "Right then. Well… enjoy the fair."

"Have a nice evening," Adam says.

We stand in silence and watch Lenny retreat into the milling crowd. It swallows him up in a holiday cheer that doesn't feel so festive anymore. I grip my snow globe box tighter. "I'm so sorry about that."

Adam puts his wallet back. "Please, Holly. Don't apologize."

"But that wasn't right," I say. "You shouldn't have to do that. He wasn't even speaking to you, not really. He was saying what he wished he could to your father."

"I know." Adam bites off his words like they're sour on his tongue. He strides off through the crowd and I'm forced to follow him. He leads us toward the quieter stalls in the back.

"Adam," I say, finally reaching for his elbow. "Wait, Adam, we don't have to leave yet."

He comes to a stop beneath an archway. His jaw works, sharp under the darkness of his beard. "I shouldn't have come here."

"No, don't say that."

"Not here. I mean to Fairhill." He runs a hand through his hair, looking away from me to the crowd beyond. "I thought it had been long enough."

"It has been. That guy was a jerk."

"No. Well, yes, he was. But he's not wrong."

"Not about what's he owed, but who he's asking it from. You're not responsible for what your father did. How could you be?"

Adam's eyes meet mine, and there's a world-weariness there I haven't seen before. "People don't see it like that. Especially not when they know I have the funds to make amends."

"Doesn't mean you have to. If you choose to, I think that's noble. You should get credit for that. Not because you *have* to do it but because you *want* to."

He nods, looking past my shoulder. "My mother and I were treated like criminals back then. By the town, by the police."

"I'm sorry about that." I shift closer, wanting so badly to give any kind of comfort. But there is none available for a wound that's over a decade old.

"Everyone asks if I know where he is." Adam shakes his head. "It's fucking humiliating to keep saying I don't."

"Not your crime," I repeat. My hand grips his forearm tight. "Adam, it was a long time ago. People here aren't thinking the same things they did back then. But the few people that are, well… screw them. Why do they matter? You're your own man, and you're a damn impressive one."

Adam looks at me for a long moment. "A damn impressive one?"

"Yes." The blush rising on my cheeks has nothing to do with this moment and my voice stays firm. "It's admirable that you're doing right by Lenny. It's not penance."

He's quiet for a long moment. "You give good pep talks too."

"Thanks. It's a skill of mine." I squeeze his forearm again. "We can leave, but promise me it's because you want to leave, and not because of him? Not everyone is terrible in Fairhill."

"No," he agrees quietly. "Not everyone."

"Hey, you two! Look up and look alive!"

I glance over to where Ginny's walking by. She's carrying a giant box labelled *cocoa* and has a smile on her face.

I look up.

We're standing beneath a sprig of mistletoe. Hung on every archway in the Christmas Fair, it's a tradition as old as Fairhill itself.

Adam sees it. "Will you look at that."

"Funny you stopped here."

"Yes." He bends his head slowly, giving me time to pull away. I don't. He presses his lips to my cheek and his beard tickles my skin. "Thank you for tonight, little Holly."

"Anytime," I whisper. "But I'm not little anymore."

His eyes are dark above me, bottomless. They feel heavy on mine. "No," he agrees. "You certainly aren't."

5 Holly

I'm a firecracker the next day.

The house is empty, my parents safely tucked away three towns over with my aunt and uncle, so Winston and I have the place to ourselves.

Well, his plans don't seem affected. He spends the day doing what he usually does, which is to watch me with his dark dog eyes from his spot on the couch. Once upon a time he'd follow me around the house.

I do morning Pilates. I shower and straighten my hair. Unnecessary? Maybe. But I keep glancing over at the house across the street and replaying the feel of his lips against my cheek, and I'm one-hundred-percent regressing to my fifteen-year-old self, minus the excessive use of lip gloss.

I also play really loud Christmas music. Mariah Carey has been the soundtrack of my morning and I've been unhelpfully belting along to her songs. On my feet are my favorite Christmas socks. They're high and fuzzy and ridiculous, with tiny bells sewn into the elastic.

I even get some work done. The document on my computer screen is full. Top to bottom, single-spaced, and it's all about Fairhill.

Adam had joked about it yesterday, but the truth is this town is interesting. I know it like the back of my hand.

There are no secret drug stashes inside ceramic Santas, but there has to be an angle. Why is it the Christmas capital of the state? How do residents here view the holiday?

I've just started writing my second page when the doorbell rings. I bounce up from the couch. "Coming!"

Winston gives a grunt as he struggles down to join me. Guard dog duty is apparently still of the utmost importance.

It's Adam Dunbar, tall and composed. His dark hair is frosted with tiny snowflakes from his walk across the street.

"Hey," he says. "Is this a bad time?"

"No, no, not at all. What's up? Need some more lights put up?"

He grimaces. "No. You did a very thorough job the other week."

"And you hate it," I say. "No, it's okay. You can tell me. Your tone sort of gave you away."

"I hate it," he says, but his voice is dry. "But I like not being the target of Maple Lane ire."

"You made the right choice. Those ladies are terrifying."

He pretends to shiver in fear. "Do you have work to do or can you play hooky?"

"I don't have to work," I say. "It is a Saturday, after all."

"Right. Want to come with me on an errand?"

I don't have to think about it. "Yes. Can I just throw on a jacket and grab my bag?"

"No," he says. "You have to leave right now, only in your sweater and Christmas socks. I have a strict time limit."

"Ha-ha, very funny. I'll be right back."

I leave Adam in the hallway and race through the house. My socks are absolutely ridiculous and I love them and not once did I think a man I was interested in would see them before he'd, you know, fallen. For me.

But now he has.

"I'm back!" I say and reach for my parka. "Where are we going?"

"It's a surprise."

"Oh, this sounds ominous," I say. "Is this when you tell me you've been a serial killer all these years?"

"I thought I told you that a couple of days ago," Adam says.

"Serial killing was my old job. I'm strictly in the programming business now."

"Quite a change in career!"

He nods. "Yes, but serial killing teaches you all kinds of skills."

"Calm under pressure," I deadpan. "Comfortable with risk. Great at tying knots."

Adam grins. "Get in the car, you dork."

"Right, right. Should I duct-tape my hands together myself or will you do that part?"

He shakes his head, still smiling, and starts the car. We drive through Fairhill and past the high school. Past Main Street and the giant diner, decorated with garish blinking lights that I love. We drive past the town square and the Christmas tree market.

Where he parks.

"We're going to the hairdressers?" I guess.

"Nope."

"The dry cleaners?"

He snorts. "I did say errand, but I wouldn't invite you along for that."

"Then where are we going?"

Adam inclines his head to the rows and rows of trees for sale. "You said you couldn't have a Christmas tree this year, because Evan's fiancée is allergic, right?"

"Right," I say.

"I have space in my house."

My mouth falls open. "Oh."

Adam's silent by my side, waiting for a response. But I don't have one. I'm overwhelmed by the idea of him offering me this. So I just stare at the rows of green pine beneath the falling snow and try not to tear up.

His voice is a bit gruff. "Good surprise? Because I don't have to have one, you know."

"No, it's a very good surprise. The best ever. Thank you, Adam."

He buttons his jacket. "Good. Well, let's go pick one out."

I drag Adam up and down the rows of trees. He insists the first one is the best, but I'm a connoisseur, and I know the merchants often put their very best ones in the back. By our third pass, it's snowing so heavily I have to shade my eyes.

And then, it appears. The perfect tree.

It's deep green with thick pine needles and it is perfectly, imperfectly symmetrical. It looks like every single tree ever in a cartoon, except for the broken tip.

Adam is nearly as tall as the tree. "This one?"

"That's the one!"

"We've walked by it three times."

"Nope."

He frowns. "We definitely have."

"Well, in that case, it didn't make itself known to us until now. Isn't it perfect?"

"It looks like all the other ones."

I shake my head. "You're a programmer, not an *artiste*. It does *not* look like all the other ones. Come on, let's lift it up."

Adam bends his knees and lifts it up with a groan. I reach for the wonky tip, but he shakes his head. "I got it."

"Sure?"

"Yeah. But let's get out of here."

Tom and his son Marshall handle the market, same as every year. They wrap our tree up. "Get home safe, Holly," Marshall says. "Looks like it's not going to stop snowing anytime soon."

"No, they've mentioned something about a snowstorm up north, right? Any chance of it coming through here?" I ask. It shouldn't affect my parent's getting home, but I can't help worrying.

"No," Adam says. White snowflakes cling to his dark hair and beard like jewels. It makes me smile, so at odds with the seriousness in his eyes. "They predicted its path at least two hours from us."

Tom chuckles. "That's the thing about the weather, son. It doesn't listen to our predictions."

Adam and I make it back to the car with the tree. It fits, just barely. The snow makes it hard for him to drive so I hold on to the tree's tip, peeking into the front seat between our seats, and give directions.

"I know my way back," Adam says.

"Yes, but it's been a while since you lived here."

"I've been back for two months."

"Turn left here."

He snorts. "I know."

"Do you have any ornaments?"

"Yes," Adam says. "I brought all of my holiday decorations with me from Chicago."

"You did?"

His mouth is quirked again. "Holly."

"Oh," I say. "I bet you have none there either."

"Not a single box."

"Were you always this evil? I remember you as Evan's nice friend."

He snorts. "Nice. That's the worst word."

"It is?"

"Who wants to be known as nice? Vanilla ice cream is nice. Not being cold is nice. Putting a USB stick in the right way round on the first try is nice."

I laugh, feeling my cheeks flame. "All right, all right. I thought you were more than nice. You were cool."

"Okay, now I know you're lying. If there was one thing I wasn't in high school, it's cool."

"You were to me. You forget, but you were older than me. You knew what was up."

Adam taps his fingers against the wheel. "I'm glad I gave you that impression, then," he says. He parks the car on his driveway and frowns, looking out the windows. "I'll have to shovel a lot of snow tomorrow."

"You don't have help with that?"

"If you know someone in Fairhill who can help, let me know," he says dryly.

"Robbie used to. That's the Sandersons' kid. But he's moved

away. Should I get some Christmas ornaments from my house? We can decorate the tree."

"Sure."

I pause with my glove on the door. "Is it okay if I bring Winston? I don't want him to be alone for that long."

"He's welcome," Adam says.

"Thanks!"

Ten minutes later and the great migration is complete. Winston had not been keen on walking through the increasingly thick layer of snow coating the street, so I'd had to carry him. Adam had helped me with one of the boxes too, asking dryly if I remembered we had, in fact, only bought *one* Christmas tree.

When it's done, Adam ends up on his two-seater couch with Winston beside him. He's lying like a sphinx, serious face gazing up at Adam.

"You've been around for a long time," Adam tells him. "You were just a puppy the last time I saw you."

"He's a gentleman in his prime," I say. "Do you have speakers around here?"

"I do. Why?"

"We can't decorate a tree without Christmas music."

Adam frowns. "I didn't say *I'd* be decorating the tree with you."

I put my hands on my hips and ignore the flutter of nerves in my stomach. "Adam, come on," I say. Saying his name feels like a luxury. "I'm not decorating a tree by myself."

"This was all for you, but I'm drawing the line at helping."

"Nope. Up you go, come on. Come here."

"Christ," he mutters.

"Yes, that's right, it's Christ's birthday soon," I say. "See, you know all about Christmas!"

Adam gives a reluctant laugh. "Fine. The tree smells good, I'll give you that."

"Victory!" I say. "He loves Christmas now!"

"I didn't say that." Adam opens one of the boxes and stares in mute horror at the glittery contents. I hit shuffle on a

Christmas playlist and the dulcet tones of Eartha Kitt crooning "Santa Baby" sound from his speakers.

Adam puts the lid down with a groan. "I regret everything about tonight."

"This was your idea, you know." I step closer and reach for one of the ornaments. Adam's hands brushes mine. We both pause, looking down at the jumble of trinkets. "This was your idea," I repeat quietly. "Thank you again. It's… really, really nice of you."

"You're welcome," he murmurs.

I twist the silver bauble around in my hand and step toward the tree. My heart is pounding in my chest, every beat strengthening my old crush. Only it feels different now. Heady and real and like something twenty-nine-year-old-me should definitely act on.

"Is it a testament to how few friends you have in this town that you're willing to hang out with Evan's little sister?" I ask. "Or a testament to how much you've missed Evan that you'll spend time with his replacement?"

Adam's dark eyes watch me hang up the bauble. "I take issue with two things you just said, actually."

"Oh?"

"Three, perhaps."

"How argumentative."

He smiles. "One, I'm not hanging out with you because I'm lonely."

"Hmm. Thanks."

"Second, you're definitely not Evan's replacement. He'd agree with that too."

I snort. "Have you forgotten how much we fought as kids?"

"No, but I also know that was a long time ago. I remember how proud he was of you."

I look down at the branch I'm decorating. Thick, surprisingly soft pine needles scrape over my skin. It feels like ages since Evan and I hung out. Between his work and his fiancée, he's busy more weekends than not, despite living only a few blocks away in Chicago. "Thanks," I say. "I know he'll love seeing you again."

Adam opens a packet of baubles. He focuses on taking them out one by one, handing them to me. But he doesn't answer.

I look over at him. "Adam?

He twists a glittery angel in large hands. "It'll be nice to see him again."

"Why is there reluctance in your voice? Something I've missed?"

Adam shakes his head, a wry twist to his lips. He hangs a bauble on the highest branch where I can't reach. "Let's just say I'm the one who let our friendship die. I haven't been great at keeping up with old friends, and he'd be right to blame me for it."

"He won't blame you. I mean, I don't know that, and maybe I shouldn't speak on his behalf. But you went to different colleges and in different directions. Friends grow apart. It happens."

Adam leans against the back of his couch, crossing his arms over his chest. Dark eyes watch me decorate the tree. "Maybe," he says. "But those ninety-hour weeks I mentioned earlier? Evan's not the only friend I've neglected."

Oh, I think. I might have hit close to home when I joked about loneliness earlier. Something clenches in my stomach. Compassion and a sudden understanding that cuts through my fantasies of his success, his attractiveness, the idea of who he is. Right to the person I've always wanted to know.

"Is that why you moved out here? To slow things down a bit?"

He sighs. "Maybe, although I couldn't have told you that two months ago."

"Why did you buy it, then?"

Adam doesn't answer right away. When I look back, he's running a hand over Winston. A lock of dark hair has fallen over his brow and hides his eyes from view. "Would you believe me if I say I'm still not sure why?"

"Yes. I'll also never ask you again if you're tired of the question. I'm sure you've gotten it all the time in the past two months."

"Once or twice," he says with a smile. "You've missed a spot over there."

"I have? Oh, you're right, it looks very empty."

I remedy that and Adam's phone rings. He gives me an apologetic smile and plugs in his headphones. I focus on decorating, but I hear the competent, commanding tones as he talks to an employee. It's not long before he's seated at the kitchen table behind me with his laptop open.

Christmas music from the speakers, a tree to decorate, and a sarcastic, handsome man to enjoy. I smile to myself as I finish up the tree. It's not in my parents' house, but it's gorgeous all the same.

I sink down onto the couch with Winston when it's done. There's only one thing left to do... and I don't want to do it without Adam.

He finally hangs up with a curt *talk to you later* and shuts his computer, coming to join me by the tree. "I'm sorry," he says with a half-smile. "I got caught up in work."

"No worries. Anything important?"

"Everything's important, if my assistant has a say in it. Look at that, then. Good job."

I grin. "Why does that sound as convincing as a parent looking at a kid's one hundredth drawing of a stick figure?"

He rolls his eyes. "Why isn't it lit yet?"

"I was waiting for you," I say. "Ready?"

"Very."

I put the plug in, and the tree lights up. A warm, golden glow emanates from the tree and fills the sparse living room. It looks like a home.

"Oh, it's beautiful." I say. "Thanks for this, Adam. I know you didn't want it, and to think you did it just so I could... thanks."

He gives me a serious look. "Anytime, Holly."

I look down at my socks. They're respectable ones. Not a

Christmas pattern in sight, the kind a mature woman should wear. "I don't mean to impose, though. I know you have work to do. An empire to run, right?"

"I don't mind," he says quietly.

"You don't?"

"No." Adam pushes off the back of the couch and walks into the kitchen. By all means it's a place he knows well, a place he grew up in. But he stops by the kitchen counter and looks at the faded cabinets. "I was going to make... well. Something for dinner."

"Something?" I say. "That's my favorite dish."

He gives me a crooked grin over his shoulder. It hits me right beneath the breastbone, hot and fluttering. "Perfect," he says. "Do you happen to know how to cook it, too?"

"Oh, you lost the recipe?"

"It didn't make it in the move."

I walk past him, letting my hand brush over his shoulder. It's like steel beneath his cable-knit sweater. "My condolences," I say.

I open the pantry and can't help myself. I start laughing.

There's a masculine sigh behind me. "I know. Pathetic."

"Is this what you live on? Boxed mac 'n' cheese and air?"

"Yes. Willpower, too."

"Of course." I take out the single packet with a grin. "Do you know something? I saw you so often online. I mean, in interviews and articles. My co-worker even wrote one about you. Well, not just about you."

"Did they?"

"Mm. It was about tech-CEO fashion."

"We're fashionable?"

I grin at him. "No. That was the point of the article."

"Ouch," he says, rubbing a spot on his broad chest. "But continue."

"Thing is, I saw all that and I thought to myself, wow. Adam has gotten so far. I wonder if he even remembers... well, if you remembered this. Ordinary life. Mac 'n' cheese in boxes." I lift it up like I've found a treasure. "But you do."

He steps closer and grips the opposite end of the packet, a finger brushing mine. "The store down the street doesn't stock caviar."

"Oh," I breathe. "Explains it."

"This isn't food worthy of trying to sweep my childhood friend's little sister off her feet," he says. "We can order in, if you'd like."

I wet my lips. "It's late. Dennis shouldn't be out in this weather."

"No, you're right. Good thinking."

"I'm okay with mac 'n' cheese."

"Yeah?"

"Yeah."

"Well," Adam says, taking the box out of my hands. "Why don't you have a seat and I'll get this show on the road."

I rest my arms against the kitchen island and watch him turn on the stove. Tall, and self-assured, and beneath all that man is a glimpse of the same teenager I had such a big crush on.

"I'll stay here," I say. "Keep you company."

6 Adam

I'm in trouble.

Correction—Holly is in trouble. At least if she continues to talk to me like this, so open and teasing and comfortable, like I'm one of her favorite people in the world. The feeling of being seen is a balm, and it isn't until it's applied that I realize how much I've needed it.

I'd dropped her back home after the Christmas Fair yesterday, and as I watched her walk up to her parents' door, there'd been a sinking feeling in my chest. *Oh shit*, I'd thought.

I want to spend more time with her. Not just in Fairhill, but back in Chicago too. I want to tease out more of her smiles and laughter. But there's no comfortable distance with her, no dates scheduled far in advance. She knows who I was, and I have feeling that she sees who I am now, too.

"This was delicious," she says and puts down her fork.

Her braid is nearly undone; golden strands escape around her face and curl over the skin of her neck. Her giant sweater drowns her form, but it suits her. It makes her look soft. Welcoming and cozy.

I wonder what she looks like beneath it.

"Adam?" she asks.

I clear my throat. "Well, you're definitely saying that to be kind."

"Nope. I haven't had it in ages." She pushes back from the table and reaches for my bowl. "Let me do the washing up, okay?"

I watch her move around the kitchen. My kitchen. The

kitchen I'd spent over a decade in before we had to leave it, from one day to the next, without so much as a day to pack. The creditors took everything, down to the necklace around my mother's neck.

I unclench my jaw and look out the window. It's darkened while we ate. The dim illumination from the Christmas lights don't reach the backyard. A gust of wind catches the house. I feel it when it happens, the wood and beams groaning.

"Wow," Holly says. "It's really coming down out there, isn't it?"

"I don't think the storm missed us."

Her hands pause in the sink, little bubbles caught on her sleeve. "Do you have a backup generator?"

"Yes," I say. "But we should prepare, just in case."

She nods. I push past her to grab two empty bottles. She takes them from me without question and fills them up with water. It's neither of our first times in Fairhill during the winter, and the town pipes had frozen more than once.

I should have prepared with more food at home.

Winston watches me secure all the windows from his throne on the couch, and when I get to working at the open fireplace, he gives a canine sigh.

"Yes," I tell him. "It is cold in here, isn't it?"

He raises the thick, furry eyebrows in an expression that looks tired. *Yes, idiot,* it says. The fire roars to life beneath my hands and I fit the screen back into place.

Outside, the wind howls.

"Holly," I say. "I don't think you should go home tonight."

She's wiping her hands on a kitchen towel. "Because of the storm? I'm just going across the street."

"I don't even think it's a good idea to open the front door right now. Look out the window. Toward the street."

Holly joins me. "Oh," she murmurs.

Beneath the streetlamps, the street is a blur of white. It whips in frenzied swirls and chaotic twists, hiding the outside world from view. Her parents' house isn't visible.

"I don't want you to go out into that," I say.

"Thank God I brought Winston over."

"Good thinking." I nod toward the roaring fireplace and the two-seater couch. "Think you'll survive an evening with me?"

I say the words casually, but my chest is tight with unexpected nerves.

Holly gives a teasing smile. "As challenging as that sounds, yes. I'll try."

"I know something that'll make it easier." I head back into the kitchen and open the top right cabinet. The bottle of old Macallan I'd brought with me from Chicago is waiting.

When I return, she's sitting cross-legged by the fire with arms braced on the sofa table. The sleeves of her sweater cover her palms. "We're drinking?"

"Have to keep warm somehow." I set down two glasses and start to unscrew the bottle. Halfway undone, I stop. "This feels wrong, somehow."

"Does it?"

"Giving Evan's little sister alcohol."

She laughs. "I'm twenty-nine, Adam."

"I know. It's been ages since this was a concern, but it just struck me." I shake my head and pour a few knuckles' worth in each glass. "I hope you like whiskey, because it's the only thing I've got."

"Mac 'n' cheese and Macallan," Holly says.

"What can I say, I'm a culinary genius." I touch my glass to hers. "Here's hoping the power doesn't go out."

She takes a deep sip and grimaces. I cover my smile with my hand, but she sees it. "It's good," she says quickly.

"Right."

"But wow. It really warms going down, doesn't it?"

"Sure does."

She takes another deep sip, cheeks heating up. "I like that part."

"Between the whiskey, the fire and the backup generator, we'll stay warm even if the power goes out."

"You're sure you don't mind? That I'm holing up here with you?"

I shake my head. "Of course not."

The Christmas music is still playing softly. It's been hours, and by now the soft crooning voices have settled into the background. It's no longer grating. The warm glow from the Christmas tree bleeds into the flickering orange light of the fire. It dances over the gold of Holly's hair and highlights the rosiness of her cheeks.

It's not awful. Not even in this house, with all its memories.

She puts her drink down and tugs at the sleeves of her sweater. "I can't believe I'm drinking with Adam freaking Dunbar."

"Hmm. Son of the town's worst offender?"

"No, no, that's not what I meant. Not at all!"

Right. She wouldn't think that, not Holly. "The founder of Wireout?" I ask, twisting my glass.

"That's not what I meant either." She looks down at her hands again, clutching them together. A fierce blush is climbing up the collar of her sweater. "I really shouldn't say. This is embarrassing, to tell you the truth."

"Is it? Now you have to tell me."

"I wish you'd had more to drink first," she says.

I meet her blue gaze and lift the glass to my lips. Still watching her, I drain it. Her eyes widen.

"And now?" I ask. "What's my reward?"

She gives a shaky smile. "All right. Well, I used to... bear in mind, I was a kid, okay?"

"Okay."

"I had a crush on you. In the past, I mean. When you lived here."

A slow smile spreads on my face. "Did you?"

"Yes." Holly puts a hand against her blazing cheek. "Ignore me, please. I suppose a small part of me is still... well, you know."

"Yes," I say. "I know."

"This is embarrassing. Say something, Adam."

I lean back against the couch. "Well, I have to tell you, I sort of suspected."

She groans and buries her head in her hands. Beside her, Winston lifts his head up and looks from her to me. There's accusation in his doggy eyes.

"It was sweet," I say. There had been a time when Holly Michaelson's shy, admiring looks had made me feel like someone.

"Adam, that's the worst possible response. Let's just forget I said anything, okay?"

"Not likely. You saw what was going on with my family. You knew, I'm sure, from Evan. But after everything that happened, you still… well. Didn't look at me different. I appreciated that."

She gives me a half-pained smile. "Thanks for saying that."

"I mean it," I say and pour myself another glass of whiskey. Draining it had been a dramatic move. "I appreciate it now too, you know."

"This? Me spilling my deepest secrets?"

I scoff and reach over to top up her glass. "Your deepest secret can't possibly be that you had a crush on me when you were fifteen. You've lived a lot since then. I want to hear about what you've done."

"Ugh, no. Because the answer is nothing. What did you mean, then?" she asks, tilting her head. "About appreciating it now too?"

I rub a hand over my neck. "How you are with me now. I don't mean to imply that you still… of course not. But you're so casual. It's nice. Talking to someone like this, you know. Extra nice considering you once knew me as a kid."

Holly recrosses her legs, eyes too knowing on mine. "Does this mean other people aren't casual around you these days? Capable of having normal conversation?"

"They are, but it's just not the same," I say lamely. I look down at my glass of whiskey and wonder just how quickly the first one had gone to my head. "Like I said, I work a lot. That's what I've been doing the past ten years. Since I dropped out of college. Before that, really. There hasn't been much time for… friendships."

"Or relationships?" Holly says. "Who do you hang out with in Chicago?"

"People," I say. "My executive team at work, mostly. A few friends in the industry."

But they wouldn't go with me to a Christmas Fair or chat my ear off in line to buy hot chocolate. And not a single one would compliment my mac 'n' cheese with sincerity.

Holly looks thoughtful and reaches up to undo her braid with quick fingers. Blonde hair spills out and across her sweater. She looks warm and soft and so beautifully ordinary, without heavy makeup or artifice. "Maybe that's the real reason you bought this house. You wanted to get away from your life in Chicago?"

I take another sip of my whiskey. It burns. "Maybe, yeah."

She smiles. "Fine. I won't push."

I lean my head back against the couch. "I still want to hear more about you and your life in the city."

"Ugh, no, you don't. There's not much to tell."

"I find that hard to believe."

She runs her fingers through her hair and combs it out. "Well, it's the truth. I went to J-school after Fairhill High."

"In Chicago?"

"Yeah. I interned at the *Gazette* and loved it. I thought my whole life would go in that direction. But it didn't. I met someone my last year of college, and he worked up in Milwaukee. We moved up there and I tried to work freelance. Newsflash, freelance is not as easy as twenty-three-year-old me thought it was."

"I'm sure it's not."

"I worked as a TA for a while, at the community college up there, too. It was okay for a few years. But the relationship went sour," Holly says with a small shrug. "Probably for the best. I had a choice between moving back to Fairhill or Chicago."

"Surprised you didn't choose Fairhill," I say. "Seeing how much you love it."

She smiles wryly. "I do love it, but I don't think I could handle living here full time. Maybe in the future, but not now. Besides, all of my college friends were in Chicago."

"So you moved back?"

"Yes. I have a tiny apartment that I rent for too much money and I have a job. I'm still doing some freelance on the side, but that's…" She gives a dismissive wave of her hand and looks down at her glass. "Difficult."

"You feel stuck," I say.

Holly sighs. "Yes. It's like I'm trying to open a door that just won't budge, you know? I've tried all kinds of keys, but not a single one fits. I've even tried a sledgehammer but the door is made from steel. So I'm wondering if I should try a different door, but every time I do, it feels like…. I don't know. Maybe I'm really close, and the next key will fit? God, I'm not making any sense."

"You are," I say. "What would you like to write about?"

Her eyes meet mine, turning passionate. "People and their problems. Actual people, I mean. Not the celebrities I'm forced to cover in shallow puff pieces. Long articles about real issues, where I get to pull quotes from experts. I want to break *real* news. I want to make people upset or emotional."

"Your articles don't make people upset?"

"Maybe about how bad they are," she says with a grin. She rests her chin in her hand, looking at me. "Am I giving you a rare look at failure?"

"You're not a failure, Holly," I say. "I told you that earlier."

"No, of course I'm not. I can decorate a Christmas tree like a champion. But the people you mentioned earlier, the ones you spent time with… well, they're not stuck behind doors that won't open?"

I run a hand through my hair and wonder how open I can be. It's been a long time since I've heard my own thoughts aloud. I don't know how they'll sound with her as the audience, echoed here in the house I never thought I'd return to. "I've had the opposite problem for a while," I say. "Too many doors open."

Holly doesn't laugh or sneer.

She just nods, eyes on me. "I can imagine."

"For years, I only focused on building Wireout. I had a one-track mind, quite literally. But then it's like I looked up one day and I was suddenly successful. Like I'd emerged in a different world. One where I was awarded honors and invited to sit on boards. Suddenly the stocks I owned in my own company weren't considered a risk factor anymore, but worth millions. Billions, now. People noticed." I run a hand through my hair, wanting to impress her at the same time as I desperately want her to not care at all about my money. Everyone else, but not Holly Michaelson. "Which door do I go into, you know? There's only so much time in life."

"I understand that," she says. "Everyone must want a piece of you, right?"

"Yes. But it's not me they want, either. It's the idea of me." I look down at my glass. "I also had a relationship end a while back. One I thought was good, but turns out it was shallow. And I realized I couldn't tell the difference anymore."

"So you sold half your company," Holly murmurs, "and moved to Fairhill."

I snort, raising my glass of whiskey to my lips. "That makes it sound like I'm having a mid-life crisis at thirty-three."

"Are you? I'm not one to judge, you know. I'm a twenty-nine-year-old woman who unironically wears Christmas socks with little bells on them."

"Ah, but that's cute. Me holing up here isn't."

She shrugs. "It depends. Judging from the lack of furniture in this place, I don't think you've made up your mind to stay. Right?"

"You're right," I admit. "This place came up on the market. You know how my mother and I were forced to leave. You and your family had a front-row seat."

"Adam…"

"It's fine. Long time ago," I say. "But when it came up on the market, I didn't even think before calling to put in an offer. I know how that makes me sound, by the way. But it's the truth. I don't know why I wanted it. A chance to see it again? To say goodbye on my own terms?"

Holly nods. She shifts closer, moving to the edge of the couch where I'm sitting. "Has your mother been here?"

"Yes. She spent an extended weekend here last month."

"How did she find it?"

I run a hand over my jaw and look at the flames. "Difficult. It's harder for her, I think. Dad's cheating and deceit. She was the one who lost a husband with no option for divorce when he fled the country."

"You lost a father, though." Holly's hand lands on mine, lying on the couch. Warm fingers brush the back of my hand.

"He wasn't that great to begin with," I mutter.

Her hand squeezes. I flip mine over, find her fingers with mine. Warmth travels up my arm from the simple touch. Holly's lips open and a soft breath escapes her. "I'm sorry," she says. "I'm not sure if I had a chance to say that, back when… it all happened. You guys left so quickly."

I look down at her hand in mine. This isn't something I've spoken about for years. Mom doesn't like to talk about it either, so it stays in a locked drawer, never to be pulled out.

Holly's a good listener. A good talker, too.

"I'm glad you came back for the holidays," I say quietly.

She shifts closer. "I'm glad you're back here too."

The lights click off and the room falls into darkness. The only light is that from the fire, illuminating the room in flickering shadows.

Holly pulls her hand from mine. "The power's gone."

As if to punctuate her words, the wind outside picks up with a howl. The entire house groans in response. "It seems like it," I murmur. "I'll check on the backup generator."

"Do you have candles?"

"Some. Should be in the drawer by the stove."

I use my phone as a flashlight and head into the basement. But try as I may, the power won't turn back on. Must be out for the whole neighborhood, then. I crouch down to get a better look at the backup generator Dad had installed. The owners who'd lived here after us had kept it.

"Shit," I mutter. They'd kept it, all right. But it was unplugged. The battery wasn't charged, because it hadn't been connected to the main power grid. Probably something to save energy in the summer months.

I should have plugged it back in come winter, but like an idiot, I hadn't. I hadn't even expected to stay here this long. I hadn't planned on spending the Christmas season in Fairhill.

But I now I won't leave anytime soon. Not as long as the blonde, funny, intriguing woman upstairs is still visiting her parents.

I grab one of the flashlights. When I return upstairs, Holly is sitting on the floor in front of the fire. Candles are lit throughout the kitchen and living room. She has Winston in her lap and her hand moves in slow strokes over the dog's fur.

We have no spare heat, we're most likely snowed in, and I only have one bed and a two-seater couch. This is going to be a long night... and I'm looking forward to every minute of it in her company.

7 Holly

"**Y**ou okay?"

"Absolutely." I give Adam a smile and pull the blanket he gave me tight around my shoulders. "I am sitting right next to a roaring fire, you know. Best spot in the house."

"You're right about that." He runs a hand through his dark hair and reaches for the bottle of whiskey. He refills both of our glasses.

I'm nervous. Can't help it, I am, nervous and excited and it's not a crush anymore. It's full-blown infatuation. "The heat might not come back on tonight," I say.

He nods. "It might not. I have more than enough wood stored inside to keep the fireplace stoked for a few days, if we have to."

"Maybe we should sleep down here." I can't look at him when I say it, patting the rug in front of the open fire.

Adam's voice is rough. "Probably the best place. Are you tired?"

"Not yet," I say. His eyes are dark in the dimly light room, a friend and a stranger at the very same time. "Maybe we should... play a game?"

"A game," he repeats. "As you've noticed, I don't have a lot of stuff here."

"You mean you didn't bring your Clue or Monopoly?"

He gives me a small, crooked grin. "Left them in Chicago."

I look down at my drink. "Maybe we can do Never Have I Ever?"

Adam gets off the couch and folds long legs beneath the sofa table, sitting at my level. The flames make him look larger than he is. Not the grown, refined man who'd gone with me to the fair yesterday. Something more elemental. Rawer.

He raises his glass. "We can play that. But I'm pretty sure I can drink more than you, little Holly."

"Hey," I say. "I thought you agreed I wasn't so little anymore."

"You're not. But it's fun to say."

I lift up my glass. "Never have I ever hated a well-loved holiday."

Adam groans and puts the glass to his lips. "You can't just say things to get me to drink, you know."

"Oh. Isn't that how the game works?"

"No."

"Whoops," I say. "Wait, then. I'll ask something else. Never have I ever... been happy about a snowstorm giving me an excuse to spend time with someone."

Adam chuckles and the sound sends a shiver down my spine. He lifts his glass to his lips and watches me do the same with dark eyes.

The alcohol burns going down my throat.

"So," he murmurs. "We've settled that, then."

"Mm. Neither one of us is unhappy about our situation."

"Not one bit," he says. "Fine. My turn. Never have I ever... had a threesome."

Neither one of us drinks. I tip my head his way, and he does the same to me. "I would have been surprised if you had," he says.

I put a hand to my chest. "I'm not a prude."

"Never said you were," he says.

"Fine. My turn, then. Never have I ever had an affair with my secretary."

Both of his eyebrows rise. "Holly, you think I have?"

I laugh, startling Winston across my lap. "Sorry, it's just one of those clichés about rich, powerful men, you know? I had to try it!"

"Rich, powerful men," he mutters. "Well, I haven't had an affair with my secretary. I don't even have one. I have an assistant. His name is Duncan and not once have I thought about him sexually."

"Bet you will after this, though," I tease. "Now that I've put the thought in your head."

Adam runs a hand over his jaw. "Christ, I hope I don't."

I laugh again. He smiles, open and free. "I like it when you laugh."

"You do?" I ask.

"Yes."

"Well, then. I'll have to keep doing it."

"Please," he says. "Now, what do I want to know? Hmm... You don't have to answer this one if you don't want to."

"Uh-oh."

"I'm curious. Never have I ever liked someone who I also had a crush on as a kid."

I put a hand over my eyes. "Adam."

He laughs. "You don't have to tell me. But I'd like it if you did."

"You're set on embarrassing me tonight."

"Not at all," he says. "I just know what I hope your answer is."

I lower my hand slowly. "Never have I ever hoped the person I just asked a question to drinks?"

He chuckles and raises his glass to his lips. He keeps his eyes locked on me as he takes a long sip of his whiskey.

"Oh," I whisper.

Then I take a long sip of the whiskey too.

Adam's lips curve into a half-smile. It's intoxicating, mingling with the heat of the drink to burn through me, branding my insides. He reaches out to brush my hair back. Featherlight fingers caress my neck.

"This might be a bad idea, but I very much want to kiss you, Holly."

My mind has short-circuited, and there's nothing but his

warm hand on my shoulder and his eyes on mine. They're so close.

I lean toward him and Adam presses his lips to mine.

My eyes flutter closed. *I'm kissing Adam Dunbar.* But then the reality seeps in, the warmth of his kiss, the steadiness of his hand resting between my shoulder blades. It's nice. It's more than nice.

He lifts his head a few inches. There's a question in his eyes.

"Yes," I whisper. My hands find the fabric of his cable-knit sweater and tug him closer. "Yes."

He chuckles darkly and lowers his head again. He kisses me slowly, unhurried and confident, like he's learning the shape of my lips and letting me learn his in return. Between him and the fire, heat blooms across my skin and settles deep in my stomach.

I'm melting.

I didn't know kisses could do that. Make me feel like I'm disappearing and existing at the same time, becoming someone new in his arms. Adam settles a warm hand on my neck. He breaks the kiss and strokes a thumb over my cheek. "Thank you, snowstorm," he murmurs.

My hands tightens into fists in his sweater. "Don't stop."

He doesn't. His lips coax mine to open, adding the dark heat of his tongue. I walk tentative hands up to his neck and slide one into his hair. The thick strands silky between my fingers.

I tug and Adam groans, low in his throat. I fall or he pushes, it's hard to tell, but then I'm lying down on the rug with him above me. Adam kisses me like we have all night. Languid and teasing and mixing light with deep. It's driving me out of my mind.

He braces himself on an arm and brushes hair from my face. "How are you feeling?"

"Great. Excellent, even." I bend a knee and brace it against his hip. "I've never enjoyed a power outage more."

He smiles and drops his head to my neck. Beard tickles my skin and then he's kissing me there, hot lips tracing a line up to my ear. I screw my eyes shut and breathe embarrassingly fast. My neck is my Achilles heel.

"Good," he murmurs. "You haven't had too much to drink?"

"Just the right amount." I pull him down and kiss him again. It's suddenly very clear to me that I won't get enough of it. Not tonight, and maybe not ever. We kiss in front of the fire for what feels like an eternity and the blink of an eye. When he lifts himself off me, my lips feel swollen and my entire body heavy with need.

"Where are you going?" I ask, pushing up on my elbows. "Adam?"

His eyes are glazed as he sweeps them down my body. Only once, and quickly, before he looks toward the kitchen. His jaw works. "You're getting cold, and it's late. I'll get bedding."

"I'm not cold," I say.

He gives me a smile that's half-apology and half-smirk. "No, but I'm getting too hot."

"Oh."

Adam disappears up the staircase on long legs and I lie in front of the fire, dazed. Had that just happened? What will happen when he gets back? Winston has the couch all to himself and is snoring softly, his gray body stretched out. "Don't wake up anytime soon," I tell him. Then I have to press a hand over my mouth to stop the nervous chuckle.

Adam returns carrying his mattress and a comforter slung over his shoulder. With some maneuvering we get the mattress stretched out in front of the fire. The screen should shield us from any flames, but the other option is sleeping in the cold house, and that strikes me as less safe.

"I only have the one," Adam says.

"One comforter? That's okay."

"I can sleep on the couch."

I give the two-seater a dubious glance. "You won't fit. The mattress is big enough for both of us."

"Right. Yeah." He grabs his whiskey and drains the glass.

My stomach is a dance of nerves and anticipation. "If you're okay with it, I mean?"

"I'm definitely okay with it."

"All right." I tell myself to be brave and reach for the hem of my sweater. I pull it over my head and instantly regret it, the skin on my bare arms getting goose bumps from the chilly air. Thank God for the camisole.

Adam turns away from me and starts to undo his belt.

How far are we going here?

I keep my socks and jeans on. It's not comfortable, but it's cold. My camisole too. But when he has his back turned, I undo my bra and tuck it beneath my sweater on the floor. There are limits to how uncomfortable I can be while sleeping.

I lie down closest to the fire and pull the comforter up.

Adam checks his phone. "It's almost eleven."

"Time to sleep, I suppose."

"Yes." He stokes the fire and then he stands there, with all his tasks completed, looking at his side of the mattress.

I scoot over to give him more room. "Sure you're okay with this?"

He gives me a smile. "Yes. But I know I'm not going to be able to lie next to you without wanting to kiss you again."

"I'm not opposed to that. I'm hoping for it, actually."

Adam groans. "You're terrible for my self-control."

"Why do you need to be controlled?" I ask and flick the cover back. "Come on."

He lies down next to me and pulls the comforter over both of us. It's immediately more cramped, but also warmer. His body next to mine is like its own power plant.

I turn on my side. "Adam?"

He's looking up at the ceiling and takes a long time to reply. "Yes?"

"Will you kiss me again?"

He sighs, but it's heated, and does just that. He surrenders to it and I surrender to him, to the deep, skilled kisses that send my pulse racing. It's not long until his hand is toying at the hem of my camisole, stroking the sliver of skin visible above the waist-line of my jeans. I knit my hands in his hair and arch my back, wanting his touch there.

Wanting it everywhere.

He kisses my neck with a groan and slides his hand up. It's warm and big along my stomach. It brushes the underside of my breast and then stops there, hand frozen against my ribs.

"Christ," he mutters against my neck. "You've had too much to drink."

"No, I haven't." I demonstrate this point rather brilliantly by slipping my hand beneath his sweater. Hard, sculpted muscle meets my curious fingers. It feels even better than it had looked the day he answered the door shirtless and sweaty.

"Holly," he murmurs. His mouth trails down my chest and finds the neckline of my camisole, stopping there. Just like his hand, just from the other direction.

Sometimes you have to take matters into your own hands.

I grip the hem of my camisole and tug it upwards. He helps me, hands gripping my waist, and I'm bared. He looks at my chest.

Thank God for flickering firelight, I think. Flames are flattering.

"Holy shit," he murmurs. Any protests are gone as he ducks his head and kisses down my collarbone. His hand weighs my breast, rubbing the nipple between his fingers.

It sends a sharp tinge of pleasure down my body.

I run a hand over his back and close my eyes. I'm feeling too much at once. Desire and need and tenderness and shyness and something I can't name, the feeling that this could be the start of something and wanting so badly not to mess it up.

His lips close around my nipple and I bury my hand in his hair. I'm not cold anymore. I don't remember what cold is. Between him and the fire, I'm burning up.

He must be too, so I grip handfuls of his thick sweater and pull. It needs to come *off*. Adam grips the collar of his sweater and tugs it over his head. It gets thrown right across the room.

The warm light of the fire makes his skin glow, deepens the shadows between his muscles. He looks like a god, a king, a warrior. I twist toward him, bending my knees so he can settle between them.

He dedicates himself to my nipples. That's the only way to describe it, as he lies across my chest and alternates between slow sucks and decisive bites that make me shiver. I grip his shoulders, the skin warm beneath my hands, and wonder if a woman has ever orgasmed from this alone.

I never have. Never thought it possible. But if he doesn't take off my jeans soon, I swear to God, I might.

"Adam," I whisper. "*Adam.*"

He releases my nipple and kisses up the sensitive skin between my breasts, returning to my neck. His hand drifts to a chaste position at my waist. "Yes?"

"I want you."

He bends his head to my shoulder and takes a deep breath, like he's trying to calm himself. But I don't feel calm at all. I slide a leg in between his and find what I'm looking for, the hard bulge in his jeans. He wants this too.

"We don't have to rush," he says, but his voice sounds strained. I rub my thigh against his length and his hand tightens at my waist.

"I know. If you don't want us to, that's fine. But don't stop on my account." I arch my back, needing his touch again. His eyes flick down along my body to where my hands are resting.

The zipper of my jeans.

His hand joins them and, almost by itself, undoes the top button of my jeans. "Tell me to stop if it's too much," he says. "We can do this tomorrow, too."

"In broad daylight?" I raise myself on my elbows and watch him slide my jeans down my legs. It's scary enough to be naked in front of this six-pack possessing, strong, confident version of Adam with the light we currently have.

He pauses with his hands at my knees. "You're beautiful," he says. "So gorgeous you have me bypassing asking you out on a proper date."

I bite my lip. "You would have asked me out?"

"I asked you to the Christmas Fair," he says darkly, working my skinny jeans over my ankles. "Endured all that fake Christmas cheer for you."

"Oh."

He lifts my leg up and kisses up my calf, my knee, to the inside of my thigh. "God, I hope Evan won't kill me," he murmurs.

"You're an adult," I say. "I'm an adult."

"Thank God for that." He stretches out beside me, finding my lips again. He kisses me with hypnotizing slowness and lets his hand stroke up my inner thigh. Higher, and higher, until it plays with the elastic of my underwear. He slips his hand beneath the fabric and strong fingers touch me. Lightly, like he's afraid I'll spook.

I breathe hard against his mouth. "Adam, please."

"Please, huh?" His fingers grow braver and every brush of his touch shoots tiny sparks of electricity through me. "Shit, Holly. You feel amazing."

I close my eyes. His hand delves deeper and he slides a finger inside. I feel vulnerable and powerful in equal measure, shy and confident.

"You're wet," he mutters. His thumb brushes over my clit and my breath hitches. He immediately does it again, finding the spot. "Here?"

"Mm."

Adam chuckles darkly and starts to circle. I'm still wearing my panties, lying on the mattress by the fire, eyes closed. Unable to think of anything but what he's doing.

He withdraws his hand and I mewl in protest, but he's not gone for long. He tugs my panties down my legs. They only make it to mid-thigh before his hand is back, teasing me. Now that he knows what I like, his fingers circle in an ever-tightening loop that makes my breath quicken.

Adam kisses me one last time before he moves down my body.

Oh. "You don't have to—"

Too late. He presses open-mouthed kisses across my skin, my inner thighs. His fingers spread and then he licks right across my clit. I groan at the pleasure-pain, my hand finding the discarded comforter and clutching tight.

Adam chuckles between my legs and settles in to work like he's never wanted to do anything more than this. Like he's discovered a new favorite toy. Never have I had a man go down on me like this.

As if I'm the one doing him a favor.

"Beautiful," he murmurs again, lips against me. Right there. I try to spread my legs but I can't, my own panties restricting me.

Adam notices. He lifts my legs up to bend me in half, giving him better access, and then he uses it.

Oh, does he use it.

I'm breathing so fast I might as well have run a marathon. His tongue, his lips and his fingers blend together until he's playing me like an instrument, my body hovering right at the edge.

"Adam," I beg, "Adam, please, I... oh my God."

He slides two fingers inside and flicks his tongue, and it's all it takes to push me over. I orgasm with his mouth on me, in front of the fire and in the middle of a snowstorm, moaning loud enough to compete with the howling wind.

Adam eventually raises his head and lowers my legs back down. He's wearing the most self-satisfied grin I've ever seen. It reminds me of how he'd smirk to Evan when he scored a three-pointer in basketball. Proud and just a little bit reckless.

But he's bearded and sculpted now, and the smile promises more pleasure to come. "Good girl," he tells me.

The words shoot through me like a shot of adrenaline. I didn't know it was my thing, but hearing him say it in his gruff voice...

Yes. Yes, yes, yes.

"Thanks," I say, which is stupid but I really mean it.

He pulls my panties back up, which is the wrong direction, and kisses me through the fabric. "No," he murmurs. "Thank you."

He lifts himself up next to me and wraps an arm around my waist, tugging me against him. As if we're done. But I can feel the hard length of him through his jeans. For all of his slow, chivalrous ways, I want him.

"What about you?"

He kisses my forehead. "I'm not going to push my luck."

I frown. That doesn't sit right with me. I'll be his good girl, but I'm also a grown woman. And I want him. So I reach for his jeans and start to undo the buttons. "You're not going to sleep in jeans, are you?"

Adam groans, but he kicks them off and settles back on the comforter. "No," he agrees. "I am going to ask you out on a date, you know. Prepare yourself."

"Looking forward to it." I turn to kiss his neck, right beneath the edge of his beard. His murmured compliments are dangerous things, and my orgasm has left me brave, and daring, and confident. So I slide my hand down his hard stomach and beneath the waistband of his boxer-briefs.

"Jesus," he whispers.

His erection is like a rock in my hand, the skin hot to the touch. I stroke him and my hand slides like silk over the hardness beneath. He's big, and thick, and I want him inside me so bad it's like an ache.

"You're playing with fire," he says through clenched teeth.

I grip him tighter. "Burn me."

Adam curses and flips me over. He grips my panties and pulls them down my legs, nudging my legs apart with his.

"Condom?"

He curses again and closes his eyes. He looks big and powerful, on his knees between my legs, the flames flickering across his skin. His erection points right at me. It makes my throat dry.

"Upstairs," he says shakily. "I'll get one."

"All right."

But he doesn't move. I nudge him with my knee and he cracks open an eye, half-smiling. "Just a second. You've got me a bit overexcited here, Holly."

"Oh," I say. "Sorry."

"Christ, don't apologize for that." He gives my hip a slap and stands up, walking across the cold room like it doesn't bother him at all.

He returns in record time and kneels between my legs again. I watch him roll on the condom in a smooth motion, no fumbling or hesitation. He strokes my thigh.

"You okay?"

"Yes."

He braces himself on his elbows and kisses me just like he had for the first time an hour ago. Slow and deep and promising. I push my hips up, but he just laughs against my lips. He's setting the tempo.

It's just so *slow*.

But when he finally reaches down to position himself, I have to hold on to his shoulders. We both groan at the feeling of him sliding into me. He's thick at the base and it burns in the sweetest mixture of pleasure and pain.

"Damn," he murmurs, and starts to move.

With every slow thrust I accommodate more of him. My body stretches and opens, until a fullness spreads throughout my stomach and makes my limbs heavy. Adam kisses me as he moves. His arms shake, and I don't think it's from his body weight.

I wrap my legs around his waist and run my nails up his back.

It seems to loosen whatever leash he has himself on. His hips slam into mine, deep and fast until all I can do is hold on, my breath coming in quick pants and his heart pounding against mine.

Adam groans when he comes, bending his head to my chest. His body is a warm weight on top of mine. I run a hand through his hair and try to catch my breath. Judging from his heavy breathing, he's doing the same.

"I'm warm," I murmur.

He chuckles. "Thank God for that, at least."

I smile down at his dark hair, wanting him to stay there forever. He doesn't. He gets up with a groan and walks toward the kitchen and a sudden shyness overtakes me. I cover myself with the comforter. The fire is down to glowing embers, darkness a blanket around us.

But Adam only left to discard the condom. He puts another few logs into the fire and lies down next to me. He gives a giant sigh and motions for me to turn onto my side. He curls himself around me, an arm around my waist. I watch the flames of the fire climb back to life and marvel at his body pressed tight behind me.

"I think you broke me," he murmurs against my ear.

"I hope not. I want that date."

"Oh, you're getting it," he says. His arm tightens around me. "I'm glad I came back to Fairhill and re-met you, Holly Michaelson."

I close my eyes and I don't think I've ever been more comfortable than I am right then. "So am I, Adam Dunbar."

8 Holly

I wake up to harsh light. Without curtains, the living room is so bright I want to shield my eyes. It's also cold, and the tip of my nose is freezing above the edge of the comforter.

The mattress is empty beside me. But Adam must have gotten up recently, because I've been aware of him all night. Lying cramped together on his mattress wasn't particularly good for sleep, but it was cozy and comfortable and I didn't mind one bit. Having him behind me, or around me, his arm over me, was the most restful thing I've experienced in weeks.

Something cold and wet licks my cheek. I laugh, pushing Winston away. Dark doggy eyes meet mine beneath two bushy Schnauzer eyebrows.

"Good morning. Sleep well?"

He jumps onto the mattress and curls into a ball where Adam had slept. He gives a victorious sigh and closes his eyes, too cute for words. I leave him be and hunt for my camisole and underwear. Then I wrap a blanket around myself and head in search of Adam.

I find him in the kitchen. His hair is mussed and he's in the same sweater, holding a phone to his ear. His eyes light up when he sees me. "Good morning."

"Morning."

"Sleep well?"

I nod. "Yes. I was very warm."

"So was I." He looks down at my bare legs and his smile widens. "I'm trying to sort out our situation," he says and gives his phone a little wave.

"Our situation?"

"With the power outage. At least the snow plowers are on their way here. You should be able to make it to your home by midday."

"My parents!" I reach for my phone, forgotten on the kitchen counter. They've left me several unanswered texts. I respond and tell them I'm okay and not to worry. Drive safe, I write too, because Lord knows how much snow there is on the roads between Fairhill and Loncaster.

Adam finds a pot in one of the cabinets and fills it with water. "Want some coffee?"

"Sure. But how will we heat it?"

He grins. "The fireplace."

Thirty minutes later and he's mixing instant coffee in a very ashy pot. I sit cross-legged on his mattress in front of the fire and admire the winter wonderland outside the windows. The back-yard is covered in a blanket of the whitest, freshest powder. It's a day to drink hot cocoa and play games. To put on a Christmas movie or decorate a gingerbread house.

Adam sits down next to me and I lean my head on his shoulder. He grows still, a hand coming to rest on my bare knee.

"Thanks for yesterday," I say.

His hand squeezes. "Thanks for keeping me company in here."

"The tree, the food, the... whiskey. All of it. I think that counts as a second date, doesn't it? With the Christmas Fair being our first."

He's silent for a long moment and my heart clenches in my throat. Perhaps that was presumptuous of me. His talk of dating yesterday might just have been caused by too much whiskey.

"Okay," Adam murmurs. "You're easy to please. I mean that as a compliment, Holly."

"Thank you?"

He tips my head back and presses a kiss to my lips. I'm acutely aware of my lack of shower and my bedhead, but he doesn't seem to care. He gives me a small smile and looks back out the windows.

I can't make out his expression.

"Do you regret it?" I ask.

"You won't let me hide anything, will you?" he says, and my heart stops. But then he wraps an arm around me. "No, I really, really don't. I just feel like I took advantage."

"You didn't," I say, my cheeks burning. "If anything, I was the pushy one. I'm sorry."

He laughs. "I was willing. You turn me on a lot."

"I do?"

"I thought that was obvious last night," he says dryly. "I want to keep seeing you. Will you let me take you out to dinner this week?"

"Yes."

"Will you come over occasionally, too? To see your tree?" He nods toward the majestic creature in the corner. "I don't know how to take care of it, you know."

I bite my lip, smiling. "Yes, I will come over. Can't let you kill the spirit of Christmas."

"Good." He takes my coffee cup and sets it down, far away from the mattress. Then he cups my jaw and kisses me. It's slow and promising and the blanket falls from around my shoulders.

He rests his forehead against mine. "I like you a great deal, Holly."

"I like you too," I whisper.

"We have hours still before the power comes back on."

"And you still don't have Clue?" I slide my hands up his neck, my voice teasing. "How will we pass the time?"

He gives me a gentle push and I fall back onto the mattress, pulling him on top of me. His smile is crooked. "No clue. How should I entertain my guest?"

"Oh, I don't know," I say. I kick at the blanket and it falls from my body. There's so much light today. All of his perfect muscles will be out... and me. But my nerves won't stop me. "You could call her a good girl again."

His eyes heat up. "You liked that, did you?"

"Yes. I don't know why, but yes."

He bends his head to my neck and I look up at the ceiling, my eyes fluttering closed. "It's so bright in here," I whisper.

He pauses. Dark hair falls from his brow onto my forehead, tickling my skin. "You're gorgeous, Holly. Fucking unreal. I could promise not to look, but I'd break it."

"Oh," I say. "Well, I guess you can look, then."

He grins. "That's a good girl."

I pull him back down.

Dating your neighbor in secret when you're living at home with your parents is difficult. It's even more difficult when said neighbor is a town celebrity and national icon, Fairhill is overrun by Christmas tourism, and Maple Lane sees dozens of cars driving through every night to admire the Christmas lights.

But the last thing I want is my parents' noses pressed to the glass of our living-room window to watch me walk over to Adam's house.

"Two cities over," Adam murmurs by my side. His hand is a warm weight on the small of my back, leading me through the restaurant. "No one should know us here."

"No one should know *me* here," I correct.

"Trust me, people don't care that much about the tech world. I'm barely ever recognized."

"I'm sure the beard helps," I say. We have a seat at a booth in the back, the most private table, just like Adam had requested for our date.

He runs a hand over his jaw. "It's a new addition. What do you think?"

"I like it. It makes you look very… rugged."

"Rugged?"

"Yeah. Manly, I suppose. Just like your… never mind."

"What were you going to say?"

"It's not important."

"No, it strikes me as very important." He lowers the menu I'm holding up to cover my embarrassed expression. "Just like my what?"

"Your chest hair," I murmur. "I like it."

"You do, huh?"

"Yes. I don't know why, but little differences like that between us turn me on."

His smile widens. "Tell me about them."

God help me, but I do. "Well, like when you have your arm over my chest, and it looks tanned and the hair on your arm is dark? Against my pale skin? I like that. Also, I can't believe I'm saying this out loud." I cover my face with the menu. "Kill me now."

Adam laughs. It's a warm sound, delighted. "Don't hide from me."

"I have to. You're probably reconsidering dating me right now. You're thinking 'Wow, she's a weird one' and you'll be driving back to Chicago tomorrow."

"Not going to happen," he says. "I have a Christmas tree to look after now."

"Right. Can't abandon your responsibilities." I peek over the menu and meet his dancing eyes.

"I like it when you tell me what turns you on," he says.

"Oh."

"A great deal, actually." His eyes drop to my lips. "I'd reciprocate, but I'm afraid I might get sidetracked if I do. I brought you here to have dinner with you, you know. Not leave after only ordering drinks and kiss you senseless in the car."

"Your car is big enough," I say. "We could do more than just kissing."

Adam groans. "Holly, I'm trying to be a gentleman."

"I appreciate it, but you don't have to be."

"I do. Because I have a feeling this might… well. I want to do things right with you. This," he says, raising a warning finger my way, "might not just be a Christmas hookup."

I dig my teeth into my lower lip, warmth spreading through my chest. "No?"

"No."

I look down at my menu with a smile, searching for the right words. I can't find any. This is going fast, and it's lovely, and the warm feeling in my chest is threatening to go to my head. "I've been meaning to tell you something, by the way. I've started writing an article about Fairhill. Like we joked about."

He puts down his menu. "You have? Tell me about it."

So I do, regaling him with the story. How it started and where it's going and the people I want to interview. He asks questions and listens, dark eyes on mine with genuine interest. In return, he talks about his work, and how much of it is so far removed from the things he'd done in the beginning. Turns out we have a lot of things in common.

Neither one of us is in a place we love.

Except right now, of course. Because there's nowhere I'd rather be than in a dingy diner in northern Michigan with Adam Dunbar. After dinner, he drives us home and parks on the Dunbars' driveway. "How are we doing this?"

I pull my cap tight over my ears and look in the rearview mirror. My parents' house is lit up like normal, so Christmassy and beautiful it makes me smile. And I can't see a thing through the living-room windows. They've drawn the blinds. We don't have an audience.

"It's a go," I say. "Run, run, run!"

Adam laughs and leads the way across the snow-packed ground to his front door. I tug my scarf tight over my face, like a bank robber. Adam looks at me and chuckles again.

We make it into his house. It's toasty warm, nothing like the past weekend, when we'd spent it together in front of his fireplace. I can't look at it without blushing.

Adam gently peels off the layers I'd wrapped my head in. "Do you think your parents would mind that much?"

I slide my hands inside the belt loops of his jeans. "No, not at all. They'd be ecstatic. That's the problem."

"Why?"

"My dad would give you his blessing to propose. Unsolicited."

Adam chuckles. "Very generous of him."

"They'd drop all kinds of hints, too."

"They're that keen to see you married?"

I shrug. "Not married, perhaps, but definitely settled. They've been together since they were nineteen, and naturally think everyone else who doesn't choose the same path is doing it wrong."

"Well, then we're doing it wrong together," Adam says. He takes my hand and pulls me deeper into the house. Despite the lack of furniture and artwork, the space doesn't strike me as sad anymore. Not with the lit-up Christmas tree and the scent of gingerbread still in the air. I'd made him bake cookies with me yesterday, over our lunch break, when I'd ostensibly taken Winston for a walk. Adam had protested, but all it took was a flick of flour his way for him to cave.

We make it upstairs and to the open door of his bedroom. The bed is in the middle, messy as usual. We'd made good use of it after gingerbread baking.

"Where are you taking me?" I say, pretend-fear in my voice.

"I just want to show you something."

"In here?"

"Yes. You said you liked something earlier."

"I did?"

He drops my hand and starts to unbutton his shirt. "Something that turned you on."

I laugh, watching him slowly reveal the smattering of dark hair on his chest. His silly side rests beneath the cool, calm exterior he shows the world. It reminds me of the Adam I knew—the Adam I'm growing to care for.

"Wow," I say. "You're putting it all out there, aren't you?"

He spreads his arms, a smile on his face. "Yes. Ravish me, Holly."

With an offer like that, how can a girl refuse?

I lie in his arms afterwards. His skin is warm and firm beneath my wandering fingers, a testament to the workouts he does daily. By daily, he means *every day*, too. Not my daily yoga routine that's more like three-times-a-week.

Spending time with him and seeing how he conducts himself chafes a little. I'm inspired and attracted, but it reminds me that I'm not living up to my potential. It doesn't sit quite right with me.

Adam's eyes are closed and his breathing is deep. Not sleeping, but near it. His tiredness after orgasming is something I find incredibly endearing.

"Adam?" I whisper.

"Mm?"

I walk my fingers across his chest and the hair I'd admired earlier. "Is your father the reason you hate Christmas?"

He doesn't open his eyes. "Great tactic, Holly. Tire a man out before you hit him with the personal questions."

"Thanks. Pretty clever, right?"

"Mmm. Very."

I press a kiss to his skin and his chest rises with a deep breath. "Yes," he says. "That's the short answer."

"Being the son of Mr. Christmas can't have been easy," I say. "I don't think people in town realized that, when they praised him so highly. Before the cops came, I mean."

"It wasn't." He finds my hand and turns it over, lifting it above his chest. My nails are painted a deep red to match the dress I'm planning to wear on Christmas day. "It was never a peaceful holiday. It was the store's most hectic time of the year."

"I can imagine."

"Every year he wanted to top the previous year's sales figures. My mom helped him, as you know. Most years we didn't celebrate at home."

"Not at all?"

Adam smiles. It's self-mocking. "We did Christmas morning until I was ten, I think. But after that they decided I was old enough to skip the pretense. My dad worked the whole day."

"He was an interesting character."

"Interesting," Adam mutters. "Yes. He was a narcissist and a cheat, and my mother made being self-absorbed an art form. They were probably the worst people for one another."

"I'm sorry. It can't have been a great household to grow up in."

He shrugs. "I had a lot of time and freedom to do what I wanted. Wasn't all bad. But Christmas? Definitely bad."

"I get why you think it's all about commercialism."

"Bigger, better, brighter," Adam mutters. It's one of Dunbar's old slogans. "What's the holiday season without a giant stuffed Santa, right? Without snow globes and lights and ten different types of wrapping paper? People go into debt for the holidays just to keep up with expectations. Companies churn out holiday movies with retired C-list actors. Hell, you can slap a candy cane on any product from November onwards and sell it at a twenty percent markup. It's ridiculous."

His voice heats up as he speaks, sincerity in every word. The roots to this run deep.

"You're right on all of those points," I say carefully. "But he left on Christmas, too, didn't he?"

Adam is still beneath me. For three long breaths, neither one of us speaks. But then he sighs. "Yes, he did. Christmas Eve, as a matter of fact."

"Just up and left?" I'd been young at the time, but not too young to overhear all the conversations. Fairhill had been filled with speculation, and there hadn't been a place in town you could go to hide from it. Maple Lane had seen more than its fair share of passersby.

I remember people showing up to their house, demanding explanations from Richard Dunbar and meeting his ashen wife and stone-faced son instead.

"I was home from college for the holidays. Not sure if you

remember that, but I was," Adam says. "He left right before the police showed up."

"Great timing."

"A bit too great, perhaps. You know the rest." His hand moves in long sweeps over my hair, smoothing it over my back. "Dunbar's was shut down a week later. All remaining stock sold in January, which is the low season. They got pennies for things he could have sold for much more ten months later. It wasn't enough to cover his debts. Not even close."

"He'd embezzled, right?"

"Yes, put everything into his private accounts. He hadn't even paid his contractors on time. He'd been counting on bigger contracts, more sales. He always needed the next season to hide his embezzlement, but eventually the pyramid scheme toppled."

"I can't believe he could leave you and your mother like that. Even now, that he can stay away."

"He'd be arrested if he came back."

"Yes, but then he'd be here. With you."

"In prison," Adam says gently.

"Yes, but still. Here. You could visit him."

"He made his choice. He left my life. Besides, he wasn't a very good father before, either."

I brace myself on my elbow and meet Adam's dark eyes. His hair is beautifully mussed, falling over his forehead. "He moved somewhere warm, right? A Central American country without an extradition treaty?"

"I think so, yes. He's only contacted me once and didn't tell me where he was. Sent a picture of a beach, though."

"How thoughtful," I say.

Adam snorts. "Very."

"That makes me feel better. Imagine, a man who spent his life building a Christmas business is now in a place where it will never, ever snow."

A smile breaks across his features. He pulls me up against him, my body atop his. Skin against delicious skin. "That's a great point."

"Isn't it?" I say. "Do you remember the last time you saw him?"

"Yeah. He was getting in the car when I got home from a friend's house. There was a suitcase in the trunk."

"Did he come clean to you? About what he did?"

"He just said he'd made some creative accounting choices and needed to lay low for a while. Might have been the under-statement of the century."

"Just a tad," I say.

He kisses me for a long, delicious while before leaning back against the pillow. He puts an arm beneath his head. "Will you tell me why you love it so much?"

"Christmas?"

"Yes. Explain it to me."

I settle back against his chest. "It's hard to put into words. All the reasons you said are great arguments against it. But I love the feeling Christmas gives you. The warm, fuzzy feelings. It's like once a year, you get a pass. You don't have to think about anything difficult. No work, no problems. You can neglect the laundry and the bills. For a few days, you get to stay inside and drink hot chocolate and wear your pajamas all day long. You're allowed to watch movies that don't make you think, they just make you feel good. It's a season that just lets you rest."

Adam makes a low humming sound in his chest. There's still skepticism on his face, but he's listening. I lift myself up on my elbow again.

"Christmas is a promise, you know? A promise that you'll have time to meet your friends again, to spend time with your family in a place where your flaws don't matter. All the decora-tions and gifts are window-dressing. They help enhance that promise, but they don't *make* it. Does that make sense? Ginger-bread is tasty, but it's not Christmas. I love Christmas trees and eggnog and turkey, but that's not the spirit of Christmas either. It's tradition and comfort and relaxation."

"Rest before the new year?"

"Yes. The food, the decorations, they're gateways to get into the mood. You're stressed, but then you smell gingerbread baking in the oven, and you think to yourself, at least there's Christmas."

"At least there's Christmas," he murmurs.

"Yes. You know, Evan and I don't live with our parents anymore. We don't live together either, of course. And work isn't always great. The year can be difficult. But you know you can always rely on the Christmas traditions, the ones you've built yourself or together with family and friends. They'll never change. So when life is shifting around you, and everything feels insecure... you'll come home and the same song is playing that you've heard all of your life, and for a little while, everything feels right in the world."

"Christmas is a comfort to you," he says.

"Yes. At least it used to."

"Used to?"

I look down at his Adam's apple. Adam's Adam's apple, I think, and it makes me smile. I run my finger over it and he sighs. "Are you trying to distract me from my question?"

"Is it working?"

"No."

"Things are different, that's all," I say. "I don't want to sound like I'm whining."

"After I just whined to you about my dad? That's a decade old news. I think you're allowed to talk about something that's bothering you."

"You didn't whine," I say. It's embarrassing to admit this, so I speak to Adam's chest and not to him. "Fairhill used to be my safe haven. I could always escape back into the past when things weren't going well in my life. With my job or my ex. But things have changed."

"Like what?"

"Evan has found the love of his life. He'll marry her, and he won't be mine anymore." I shake my head. "God, I hear how that sounded. I don't mean it like that. Just... we've been so close over the past decade. Closer than we ever were as children. But he's not that person anymore when she's around. He belongs to her first, and his family second now."

"But she's nice."

"Oh, Sarah's the best. Really. But she's perfect for Evan now, you know? Not for Evan in the past. And so Evan can't be Evan of the past around her." I sigh, turning over onto my back. "And then there's the pine allergy."

"Right. What a bitch."

I nudge him with my knee and he laughs. "Just kidding. What else?"

"Well, Winston is dying. Not at this very moment, I mean. But it's coming and he's getting old and I have no idea how I'll cope when he goes."

Adam makes a deep humming sound in the back of his throat. The thought of Winston makes my voice tremble. "I know I've said I feel stuck in my job, but the truth is I hate it."

"Ah."

"My boss is an asshole who doesn't respect weekends. My co-workers bend over backwards to get promoted and don't like to help one another, because they see everyone as competition."

His voice holds a smile. "You would hate that environment."

"I do. I really, really, really do. I used to love writing and now I can't bear to write another article about failed Botox injections."

"Fascinating stuff."

"No, it's not."

"Things are changing around you," he says, "but not for you." He lifts himself onto an arm and looks down at me. The comforter has slid down to his waist, revealing the strong muscles of his chest. "I understand that. I'm so damn tired of Wireout. I know I'm not supposed to say it, or even think it. It sounds ungrateful. But I am."

"That's why you came here?"

"Yes. I wanted to get back into this house on my own terms, yes. But I also needed out of the place I was in."

I turn on my side and look up at him. He looks thoughtful,

and reserved, and open. All at the same time. "What happened back in Chicago?"

His lips curve. "You're good, you know. Have you ever thought about being a journalist? Interviewing people for a living?"

I chuckle. "No, what a great idea!"

"I'm full of them." He bends his neck and kisses me for a long time. My fingers slide into his hair.

"Good tactic," I murmur. "But I won't forget my question."

He gives a playful groan and buries his head against my neck. "You'll get the scoop no matter the cost."

"Extra, extra, read all about it."

Adam smiles. I feel it against my skin. "All right. A relationship ended."

"Oh," I say. His confession knocks the wind out of my sails. He'd been in a serious enough relationship that he had to leave the city. Take some time for himself.

Jealousy burns in my chest. It's irrational, sure, but undeniable.

"Not something I want to bring up in bed with you," he says.

"No, no, I was the one who asked."

"And you wouldn't take no for an answer," he says. There's teasing in his voice, a warmth that soothes the jagged feeling inside. But then he keeps going. "We were together for a pretty long time, but in the end it didn't serve either of us. I mentioned it to you. It felt shallow."

"How long?" I murmur.

"Two years, I think." Adam braces a knee between mine, aligning our bodies with one another. He carries his own weight but puts just enough on top of me to make me feel deliciously covered. I'd told him I liked that yesterday. Whispered it after sex, actually, when he'd done just that.

Now he's using it against me.

"What about you, Holly?" he says. A big hand brushes hair back from my forehead. "You're kind and funny. Smart. Drop-dead gorgeous, too. Is there someone for you back in Chicago?"

"No, not really."

"Not really or no?"

I nudge him with my knee again and he kisses me. It's an apology and a question.

"No," I say. "I dated someone briefly but it ended over the summer."

His lips travel to my ear. "Interesting."

"Interesting? That's what you're going to say?"

Adam laughs. It's a rumble through his chest, travelling into me. I feel surrounded by him, covered by him, and more infatuated than I've ever been before. "Yes. You know, I'll be back in Chicago for the new year. I don't think I can hole out in Fairhill for much longer."

My heart is beating a war drum in my chest. "Funny. So will I."

"Counting on it," he murmurs. "Why do you think I want to go back?"

9 Holly

I hear my brother's car pull into the driveway.

"Holly!" Dad calls. "Evan's home!"

Three seconds later, Mom's voice rings out from the bedroom opposite mine. She's been wrapping gifts out of our sight for the past half hour. "Holly, Evan just pulled up!"

They're like two heralds, announcing the arrival of their favorite child. I roll my eyes and save the document I've been working on. The article has taken on a life of its own. The words have poured out of me, observations about Fairhill's Christmas spectacle. My working title is a question inspired by Adam. *Is Fairhill a holiday destination fueled by true Christmas spirit or rampant commercialism?* It's led me down a rabbit hole of town history, not to mention the origins of Christmas traditions and themes. Not a single newspaper might want to run this article.

But for the first time in months, it's one I want to write.

I head down the stairs just in time for Evan to open the front door. "I'm hooome!" he bellows. He has a stuffed gym bag in one hand and a bouquet of fresh flowers in the other. He hands them to Mom, who wastes no time in getting teary-eyed. Winston barks joyously at his feet, tail wagging.

I'm third in line for hugs. When it's my turn, Evan lifts me clean off the floor.

"Flowers?" I ask in his ear. "Kiss-ass."

He answers loudly. "Thank you, Holls. It's always a pleasure to set a good example for you."

When I'm safely back on my feet, I aim a kick his way. He

sidesteps it and pretends to swing an upper cut. Winston gives a warning bark at our feet.

"Already fighting," Mom says, but there's joy in her voice. "Now we're all home for Christmas. Was the drive okay, honey?"

Dad reaches for Evan's bag. "Let me take that."

I follow behind my fawning parents and Evan's tall form. He looks great. Happy and healthy, with the circles under his eyes from the past summer gone. His dark blond hair is cut neatly and curls at his nape. He's even wearing a button-down shirt.

This is my brother, the same guy who'd worn a *Star Wars* shirt for two weeks straight in middle school and refused to let Mom wash it. His apartment had been littered with takeout boxes for most of our twenties.

Sarah's influence on him is astounding.

I make him a cup of coffee in the kitchen and listen to my parents quizzing him about the trip, the past week, his plans the coming week, how Sarah is doing, and how work is. He endures the debriefing session with more patience than I had.

I drop my big piece of news as soon as they fall quiet. "They've moved the Christmas Fair!"

"They've done *what?!*" Evan says. Finally someone who reacts the way one should to the changes around here.

"There's actually been a lot happening," Mom says. "Not just in town, either, but right here on Maple Lane!"

"Your old friend is back," Dad says. There's anticipation in his voice, and I can picture the joy in his eyes at being the one to tell Evan the big news. He beat Mom to it. "Adam Dunbar has bought the house opposite ours. He's here right now."

There's a beat of shocked silence. "He's *here*? Adam?"

"Yes. I texted you about it," Mom says. "But you didn't react."

"I thought you were joking. Not a very funny one, sure, but I couldn't imagine you were serious. Adam Dunbar back in Fairhill? Wow."

"Holly has been spending time with him," Dad says. "Holly!"

I join them with two coffee cups, sliding across the wooden floor on my Christmas socks. Evan's eyes are wide. "You've spent time with Adam?"

"Yeah. He doesn't really have any friends in town. Coffee?"

"Thanks." Evan scoots to the side on the couch and I sit down next to him. "So? How is he? Also, how the hell have you kept from texting me about it?"

I ignore the last question. "He's the same, I think. You knew him better than I did." I take a sip of coffee and it scalds my tongue.

Not like I ogled him every chance I had as a teenager.

"Yeah, but he's not the same these days. He's a billionaire." Evan's stunned proclamation fills the space. "I mean, I think I was the last person who texted. Seven years ago, maybe. He was always busy."

"He's still pretty busy. But he wants to see you," I say, and immediately feel disloyal. I don't know Adam's thoughts. He seems reluctant when we've spoken about it, as if Evan would somehow dislike us being together.

Not that I have any idea how to tell my brother about that. I don't even know what we are, not really. It's too early.

"Huh," Evan says. "What have you two been doing? I don't know if I'd know how to talk to him these days. He lives such a different life from us."

"He's the same person," Mom says. "I speak to him all the time!"

"You yell at him from the driveway," I say.

She shoots me an affronted look. "We talk. Just the other day I asked him how he fared during the snowstorm. He said he did all right and that you two looked out for one another. I thought that was sweet. Did you communicate across the street with flashlights?"

"Morse code?" Dad says with a chuckle. "You and Evan were obsessed with that, remember?"

"It was one family holiday," I say.

"Yeah, and Holly never got the hang of it," Evan says.

"Only because you hogged the code book."

He snorts, grinning into his coffee cup, and I can't help but smile. He's here, and we have a few days until Sarah joins us. Plenty of time for some old-school sibling shenanigans.

"Anyway, he's very nice," Mom says, like she didn't hear our little interlude. "Not stuck-up at all, even if he's worth more than Fairhill."

"Mom, think bigger," Evan says. "He could buy the state."

Dad chuckles, and there's pride in the sound. "Who knew he would become so successful? When he sat at our kitchen table, doing homework with you two?"

"Not me," Evan says. "What have you been doing with the boy genius, Holly? He already knows the town."

Three pairs of eyes are on me, and in my mind, I see him naked beneath me. "Oh, you know," I say weakly. "The usual."

"The usual?"

"We went to the Christmas Fair."

"That's not all," Mom says. She's practically grinning. "They went out to lunch the other day too. I saw you two, driving away in his car."

"Yes," I say, nodding quickly. "We've also had lunch."

Just lunch.

"They're really getting along," she continues. "Is he single, sweetheart? Because I think you two would make a beautiful couple. Just beautiful. Imagine the children, Craig."

Dad rolls his eyes, but he doesn't look displeased. He's smiling beneath the hand he runs over his jaw.

The protest comes from Evan. "Mom, be serious. Adam Dunbar isn't going to date Holly."

"Why not? Your sister is amazing!"

I keep my face carefully blank and take another sip of coffee.

"Yes, she is," Evan says. "Holly's the best. But he's dating some influencer."

Mom shakes her head. "Absolutely not. He hasn't had any visitors, except for his mother. We would have seen that."

"First of all, that's stalkerish behavior," Evan says. He turns to me for backup.

I give a hurried nod. "Oh yes. Stop peeking behind the curtains."

"Exactly," Evan says. "Secondly, Sarah follows his girlfriend on social media. Her name is Vienna something, I think. She does a lot of... I'm not sure, actually. Something with clothes or makeup. She said they were on a break, but still together." He sighs. "Honestly, I can't believe I know that. But Sarah tells me anything she finds out about Adam, because she knows we were friends."

"Huh," Mom says. She looks like I feel.

Shocked.

But then she shrugs and gives a cheeky smile, looking straight at me. "Well, it isn't over until he has a ring on his finger. A break isn't a good sign. Get in there, Holly!"

I try my very best to smile. A wet nose presses against my hand and I look down. Winston rests his head on my knee, dark doggy eyes looking up at me. I run my fingers over his soft, velvety ears.

He's on a break with his girlfriend.

Which explains why he fled to Fairhill. He needed space away from her, or she needed it from him. Just like he'd said. But it's just a break.

And breaks always come to an end.

Evan's arm drapes around my shoulder. "What do you say? Do you have time for Monopoly tonight? I'll kick your ass."

I give him my best smile. Playing a few rounds with our old set is a Christmas tradition. The cardboard is coming apart at the seams and it's missing all twenty-dollar bills, but none of us would buy a new version.

It's my favorite holiday. My family is all back together again.

And I'm not going to think about Adam's potential girlfriend.

"Yes," I say. "But you're the one who'll lose."

I make it past Monopoly and evening hot chocolates. I make it all the way to my bedroom, saying a cheery goodnight to my family, before I dive onto Google.

Somehow I must have missed her when I looked him up earlier, this mysterious influencer girlfriend. But now that I know who to look for, I find her immediately.

Seeing her images throws me into a pit of despair.

She's gorgeous. Slender and willowy and with a big, artificially whitened smile. Every single one of the pictures on her social media looks perfect. Like she travels with a personal photographer.

Maybe she does, for all I know.

The amount of followers she has, too... let's just say it's more than the population of Fairhill. A good deal more. Adam could buy the state and she could populate it.

There are subtle hints of him in her pictures. Never his face, but he's there. It's easy to imagine who took the picture of Vienna posing in a bubble bath with the Chicago skyline behind her. She posted a picture of her brunch eight months ago, and across from her is a long-fingered, masculine hand curled around a cup of coffee.

I know that hand.

I've seen it on my skin.

I throw my phone away. It bounces on my comforter, unharmed.

This is who he dates when he's not taking a few months for himself in Fairhill. This is the life he lives. I've seen the hints of it. The expensive car, the area where he lives in Chicago, the magazine that interviews him. Adam is not the Adam he once was. And that's fine. It's great. He's so much more now.

But I'm not. And I've never felt more aware of that than right now, with my career going nowhere, my irregular workout schedule, my tiny studio apartment and my credit card debt. I press the heels of my hands to my eyes and try not to cry. This is not worth crying over.

But my body doesn't know that, and the emotions Adam has made me feel have been too strong. I have no defenses left.

"It's okay," I murmur, focusing on taking deep breaths. "Nothing's changed. You don't actually know anything."

But I see his girlfriend in my mind's eye and hear my brother's words. *They're just on a break.*

I'm the same infatuated girl I'd been as a teenager, hopelessly in love with my brother's best friend. Spinning fantasies out of thin air and building a future out of a few smiles.

My phone chimes with a text. I take a deep breath, in and out, and consider ignoring it. Going to sleep right away. Draw my drapes and ignore the house on the other side.

But I don't. My hand shakes, gripping my phone.

It's him.

Adam: Hey. I take it Evan's home? Hope you guys had a good evening catching up. I know you've missed him.

The words feel blurry on my screen. It's so polite, the tone almost formal. Is this the way he texts with his girlfriend? Or am I the acquaintance he's also enjoying over the holidays?

Another message appears.

Adam: I won't bother you in the coming days, I know it's family time. Let me know when you're free. Would love to see you.

I put my phone on airplane mode and put it on charge at the far end of my room. Then I turn off the lights and crawl into bed, pulling the comforter up to my nose, and try to think of nothing but the Christmas movies I'll force Evan to watch with me tomorrow.

I'm not very successful.

The next day, Mom has made us all a giant family brunch. We

eat for at least an hour and a half, with the occasional break to fry more bacon or another egg. Evan eats like a beast and I tease him about it. He takes that as an invitation to show off his biceps.

"You're such a teenager," I chide him. He reaches over with the newspaper and swats my shoulder.

"Sorry. I think I saw a fly."

I stick out my tongue at him.

He grins. "And who did you call a teenager?"

We're reverting to our old dynamics, finding our balance, and it feels good. It feels right. It's like the traditions I told Adam about. The small consistencies that keep the world familiar amidst the chaos of life.

Evan takes off with Mom to do some last-minute Christmas shopping, and I spend the day with Winston on the couch, working on the article. Watching the sparkle of snow outside the window.

Ignoring Adam's texts.

That's how I spend the evening, too. Petting Winston's soft ears and watching him ignore my brother's attempts at playing. "I guess he's not interested," Evan says, but he's frowning. The toy he's holding had once been Winston's favorite.

"He's been very tired the last few days," I say. We play charades that night, using an app I've downloaded for my phone. The categories are up-the-wall. Watching Dad trying to act out song titles might be the most I've laughed all year. A man over sixty should not be trying to act out "Smack That" in front of the fireplace, but he does, and the rest of us howl.

The next day Adam sends me another text.

This time it's a picture of the Christmas tree. It looks beautiful and green and full, and he's lit it despite the sunlight streaming through his windows.

Adam: The tree is still alive and well. Thought you should know I haven't killed it (yet).

My fingers fly over the keyboard before I stop myself, my heart in my throat.

Holly: Is that a threat?

He replies right away. So close, just across the street.

Adam: Just trying to hedge my bets.

Adam: How's your day been so far?

I tuck my phone into the back pocket of my leggings. The pocket is the second-best thing about them, right after the blue reindeer pattern. I know I should answer. But I'm afraid of asking the question, afraid of hearing the answer, afraid of what it'll mean.

"I'm baking pecan pie," Mom says. "Want to help, Holly?"

I give her my brightest smile and throw myself into Christmas preparations, running from difficult conversations.

The kitchen smells delicious a few hours later. I can hear Dad and Evan argue about how to best keep the fire stoked in the living room, and I close my eyes, feeling whole for the first time since I heard the news about Adam's girlfriend.

I have this. Whatever else happens, I have this.

"When is Sarah coming?" Mom asks, leaning against the doorjamb to the living room. "Tomorrow, right?"

Evan's voice is warm. "Yeah, she's taking the bus. She feels really bad about not getting more days off."

"No, no, she shouldn't. We're so grateful she could come at all," Mom says. "Next year we should invite Sarah's parents here, too."

"Thanks, Mom," Evan says. There's patience in his voice, one that belongs to a man who's spent the past months navigating wedding prep, engagement parties and the slow merging of two very different families. He stops in the door to the kitchen and looks to Winston' food bowl. "Who gave the dog food last?"

"I did," I say. "But it was hours ago."

"He hasn't touched it."

We all look at the kibble accusingly. It's still there.

Something sinks in my stomach, and I have to swallow against the lump in my throat. Everyone knows what happens when a dog doesn't want to eat anymore. When he doesn't want to play or go on walks.

Mom wipes her hands on her apron. It's a nervous gesture, but her voice has the same command I'd clung to as a child in times of trouble.

"I think we should see if Dr. Shelley is free tomorrow. Better to go to the vet one time too many."

Evan meets my gaze. "We'll all go," he says.

10 Adam

Something's off.

It's two days before Christmas, and Holly isn't talking my ear off about how excited she is. She isn't sending pictures of the gingerbread house she was planning to decorate, even though she promised to last week. I haven't seen her leave her house much, either, even if I hated becoming like the Martha Sandersons on Maple Lane who watched their neighbors' life as if it was the most captivating TV.

But worst of all, she isn't answering my text messages.

I'd met Evan yesterday. We had gone for coffee on Main Street at the same diner he'd once worked at over summer break. It had been nice. Cordial and hesitant, like two people trying to get to know one another again.

I know I'm the reason for that hesitancy. I'm the one whose trajectory isn't normal, isn't what people around here expected. There'd been curiosity in his voice, but he'd also sounded on his guard.

I fucking hated that.

It reminded me of how Holly sounded the first day. But then she'd dropped that, as if she'd seen that I was just the same Adam she'd always known, beneath the years and life changes and the fancy car that makes me stand out like a sore thumb in Fairhill.

I hadn't asked him about Holly. He hadn't volunteered any information. But it had been there on my tongue. *Why is your sister ignoring me?*

So here I am, sitting on my couch in my empty house, and

staring into the fire with my phone in my hands. She's busy. She has family. It's natural that she has no time for me at the moment. Christ, it's the holidays, and I know what that means to her.

But her silence is so unlike her that I can't resist.

Adam: Hey. Is everything okay?

I look down at the text, and suddenly, my life here doesn't seem like a fanciful escape from Chicago anymore.

It feels like I've been on the run. Trying to ease the wounds of the past with this house, when the truth is the past will never change. Dad will never come back. Mom doesn't want to spend Christmas in this house, not to mention this town. Not after the way some people treated us after Dad's business collapsed.

I look around the living room. Memories interpose on one another, past and present. Some good. Some bad. And some laced with bitterness.

It's time to let go of it. Both my old life here, and the dissatisfaction I felt with Wireout. It belonged to this year.

I won't carry it with me into the new one.

I spend the rest of the evening on my laptop, answering emails. Somehow that had become the better part of my working days. Once, it had been programming, creation. Refining the product and the app. I'd been right in the action. Now I'm a glorified executive… and I hate it.

My phone chimes with a text.

Holly: I'm sorry. I've been a bit of a mess today.

I close my laptop and reach for my sweater. I pull it over my head and walk to the front door. Feet into boots, coat on. It's freezing outside.

But this is the first time she's responded to me in days.

Adam: Tell me what's wrong.

I write it crossing the street. Most of the houses on Maple Lane are dark now, the hour late. Blinds are closed and doors shut. The streetlamp casts a ghostly glow over the snow-clad ground. I look around, but there's no one around to see me walk onto the Michaelsons' front yard.

I scoop up a handful of white and shape it into a snowball. It's not hard to know which window is hers. I've been in this house, even if it was over a decade ago. Hers is the only bedroom with a light still on in the window.

I feel like an idiot.

I also feel more alive than I have in years.

Pulling my arm back, I lob the snowball at her window. It hits with a dull thud.

It takes Holly a few seconds to look out, and by then I have another cold chunk of snow in my hand. I grin up at her. Any second now, and her parents might wake up. I feel like a teenage boy again.

"Adam," she mouths. I can't hear her, but her lips form my name. I'd recognize it anywhere. I lift up my phone and make a show of typing.

Adam: Come out and tell me what's wrong.

Holly shakes her head. I can see it, long and blonde and cascading over bare shoulders. She's only wearing a camisole.

Seeing her feels like a balm after the past days of unexpected distance. Over the two weeks she's been back in Fairhill, she's become a necessary part of my life here. The one person I want to talk to most in the world. Perhaps that should scare me, how quickly she's gotten beneath my skin.

But all I want is to pull her closer still.

Holly: It's freezing!

Adam: I'll keep you warm.

She looks down at me, and I see the exact moment she gives in. A soft smile spreads across her face and my heart stutters in my chest. She's saying yes, continuing to want me the way I want her.

Holly holds up a finger and I nod. I'll wait.

A minute later she opens the front door carefully. She tiptoes out in winter boots, pajama pants and a thick jacket. Her hair is a golden halo beneath the streetlamp. "What are you doing here? Have you gone insane?"

"You said you weren't feeling good," I say. "What's wrong?"

She wraps her arms around herself. "We had to take Winston to the vet."

My heart sinks. "Oh, Holly. What happened?"

"He wasn't really moving around, he didn't want to play… I mean, that's been going on for a while, but now he stopped eating too."

"What happened?"

"He's okay," she says, voice heavy with relief. "The vet wasn't available until today, so we were all fearing the worst, but… Adam, he just had a toothache."

"A toothache?"

"Yes. I never thought of dogs getting abscessed teeth. He's home now, but a bit groggy from having been sedated." She shakes her head, cheeks flushing with cold. "I was convinced this was it. We all were. Driving there… I think we were all afraid we weren't coming home with him again."

I put my hands on her shoulders and grip her tight. "I'm sorry. I know how much he means to you."

Holly nods, rocking back on her heels. "It was scary."

"I'm sorry," I say. "Is that why you've needed some time?"

"Yes." She looks down at the snowy ground between us. "But Adam, it wasn't the only thing."

"Oh." From the way she's worrying her bottom lip, she's nervous about saying the next part. It makes my stomach sink. Does she want to end this?

"Evan told me something the other day," she says.

"After him and I met up?"

"No, earlier. He mentioned something his fiancée had seen online. Apparently she follows your girlfriend on social media? God, just saying this out loud sounds stupid." She takes a deep, fortifying breath, her warm exhale a plume of white smoke in the freezing air. "Your girlfriend has said publicly that you're just taking a break. That you're still together."

Everything inside of me grows very still. I meet Holly's beautiful, hesitant, insecure gaze, and I know what I say next matters. It matters a lot.

But what comes out is something completely different.

"Fucking Vienna," I say.

I must have raised my voice, because Holly looks back at her dark house. Her hand finds mine and she pulls me away from the front door, over to the shed. Our feet crunch in the snow. "What do you mean?"

"We *aren't* on a break. Or if we are, it's a permanent one. I'm not dating her anymore. To tell you the truth, I should have ended it a lot earlier than I did."

"You ended it?"

I nod. There's no one I want in this moment with us less than Vienna, but here we are, and I need to erase that look on Holly's face. The hesitation and the pain in her eyes. Like she has one foot out the door, ready to run.

"We've never been on a break. If she's still going around saying that on social media… Christ." I run a hand through my hair and find it cold and stiff. "She took the break-up hard, I think. She called me a lot after. Made weird remarks publicly."

"So it's not true?"

"Not in the least. I'm sorry if it spooked you."

She shakes her head. "No, I'm the one who spooked for nothing. I should have asked you about it. I should have asked… oh, Adam. What are we doing here, really?"

"We've been getting to know one another again."

"But what happens after Christmas? When we're not neighbors anymore, away from Fairhill?"

"I like you a lot," I say. It's the truth, and I want to be as honest with her as she's always been with me. Right from the beginning. "This wasn't expected, but I'm happy it happened. I want to keep seeing you in Chicago."

"You like me now," she whispers. "But you won't once you've seen my regular life."

I raise an eyebrow. "Why do you think that?"

"Because I don't have everything together."

"Holly, you haven't given the impression that you do right now, either," I say, unable to hide my smile. "I don't need you to have your life sorted out. I don't."

She gives me a withering look that makes it clear she thinks the opposite. I chuckle and step closer. The thick material of her jacket hides her shape, but I put my hands on her waist. "I'm sorry. I shouldn't joke around right now."

"But it's true," she says. "I am a mess, and you're... you. You exercise while you're taking meetings!"

I tip her head back. "Holly, I've spent a decade avoiding messes. Perhaps it's time I stopped doing that."

Her exhale warms the air between us. "Oh."

"Besides, I'm the real mess," I say. "It won't always be easy, spending time with me. Reporters might ask you questions, there will be some... media coverage. My life hasn't been ordinary for a long time. Dealing with me won't be either."

"You're worth it," she says.

I smooth my thumb over her cold cheek. She's so beautiful beneath the streetlamp that it aches to look at her. "You've helped me realize what I want."

"I have?"

"Yes," I say. "I want a life where I don't work sixty hours a week. I want to let go of the bitterness." I find her bottom lip, full and warm beneath my fingertip. "You're the realest thing I've had in my life in a very long time."

"Oh."

"Let me take you out on a date in Chicago, Holly," I say. The word *please* hovers on my tongue. Her warmth over the past two weeks has felt like seeing the sun again, the heat, and it's seeped into my bones. I can't imagine the future without it.

Her lips curve into a small smile. "You really want to keep seeing me after Fairhill?"

"God, yes."

She rises up on her tiptoes and presses warm lips against mine. It's the sweetest taste, infinitely precious, and I kiss her back beneath the falling snow. Pull her as close to my body as our heavy winter jackets allow.

When she finally pulls away, her voice is shaky. "Adam, Adam," she says. "What are you doing for Christmas? Is your mom coming?"

I shake my head and bend to nuzzle the side of her neck. She smells sweet, like shampoo and some Christmas spice. Nutmeg or cinnamon, perhaps. Maybe she's been baking. "No. She's celebrating with her new partner, down in Chicago."

Holly locks warm fingers behind my neck. "Come to our house. Please?"

"I couldn't impose like that."

"You wouldn't. Mom and Dad would be thrilled, Evan and Sarah would love it."

"And you?" I ask, brushing my lips over her jaw. "Would you love it?"

"Yes. Please, Adam. I promise it'll be nice, even if you don't like Christmas."

"If you're there," I say, "how could it not be?"

"And Duncan?"

My assistant pauses on the other end of the line. "Yes?"

"Merry Christmas. Take some time off."

"Um, yes. Thanks, sir. Enjoy the holidays."

I click off the call and grin at the shock in his voice. That's three times in one phone call. First, when I briefed him about my return to Chicago after Christmas. Second, when I told him I'll decrease my workload next year. He'd laughed, as if I'd told him a joke, before realizing I meant it. Wireout doesn't need me anymore, not the way it did in the beginning.

It's time to find a new passion.

I put my phone in my pocket and walk across the living room. This place is going on the market next year, too. It's given me what I needed. What I'd craved for years and never gotten. Closure, by realizing that I'll never fully get it. Yesterday I'd emailed Lenny and asked him for the names of the other families my father cheated out of their income.

I'll pay all of it back.

Holly had been right. I don't have to do it, and it's not my responsibility… but someone has to take it. If it's not going to be my father, it might as well be me. Those people had suffered the consequences for long enough.

Embracing the spirit of Christmas, I think wryly. Holly would be proud.

I grab the giant bouquet of flowers from the kitchen counter and the bottle of champagne I'd picked up. In my back pocket is the gift I've prepared for Holly. I won't admit it, but I'm nervous. What exactly is the protocol when you go to your neighbor's house, which also happens to be the family of your childhood best friend? Where you'll also meet the parents of the woman you're dating?

Sure, I've met them before, but not since I discovered their daughter is the woman of my dreams.

I make it across the street and knock on their door.

Evan is the one who opens. "Hey, man. Come on in. Merry Christmas."

He ushers me into a house buzzing with activity. The kitchen table has been extended into the living room and is beautifully decorated with a garland of pine along its center. The scent of food hangs thick in the air, and from the living room comes the sound of Christmas music.

I meet Mrs. Michaelson first. She surprises me by giving me a hug and accepts the flowers with a delighted smile. "Thank you! Such manners, Holly, come see this. Adam brought us flowers!"

I rub my neck. "Thanks for having me, Mrs. Michaelson. Merry Christmas."

"Oh, call me Jane," she says. Her hands are busy arranging the flowers in a vase. "We're all so happy you could make it. The more the merrier, just like the season's all about."

Holly appears in the doorway. She's in a deep-red dress that hugs her curves and her blonde hair is gleaming over her shoulders. She's even painted her lips red, and my stomach twists with desire. "Hello," she says.

"Hi, Holly."

She smiles back, a small and intimate one that makes my chest tighten. "We're having mulled wine in the living room. Want to join us?"

"Yes, thank you." It takes effort not to pull her close, sling an arm around her waist or kiss her temple.

Evan introduces me to his fiancée Sarah. She's a diminutive brunette with a shy smile, her voice a bit shaky when we shake hands.

"Congratulations," I say, motioning to her left hand. "Evan told me about the engagement. Have you set a date?"

Evan pulls out a chair next to him and I have a seat. We talk about their upcoming wedding, and I'm trying to focus on the conversation. But it's hard when Holly is sitting right across from me on the couch. So chaste, so proper, but she's smiling into her mulled wine. I haven't kissed her yet.

It feels like a crime.

"Oh, look at that," Mr. Michaelson says. "He wants to say hello."

I look down at the dog sitting by my knee. Winston's tail is thumping against the rug. "Hello, buddy." I rub a hand over his head. He's wearing a red bowtie around his neck. It makes me smile, knowing without a doubt who's responsible for it.

"I heard he had some trouble this week?"

"Oh, yes," Mr. Michaelson says. "He gave us all a scare, didn't he?"

The family tells the story and I listen to it, enjoying as one topic drifts into the next. There's no stress in their voices. No tension. No one is waiting for a phone call to pull them away.

The house is decorated to the nines, but everything is... personable. Aged. I spot a Santa missing half a beard. Jane catches me eyeing it and chuckles. "Holly made that when she was eight," she says. "We've displayed it every year since then."

"It's beautiful."

Holly laughs. "Liar."

"You were artistic, even then," I say.

"You're digging yourself deeper," she warns, smiling at me across the living room. I hold up my hands in surrender and have to bite the inside of my cheek to keep from grinning. I'm halfway to head-over-heels for this woman.

Okay. A lot more than just halfway.

We head to the dinner table as the evening progresses. It's nice and warm and friendly, with the family joking and teasing one another. They extend a hand to me and Sarah regularly, inviting us into the conversation, asking us questions.

Mr. Michaelson is the one to thank us all for coming. His voice is warm as he looks around the table. "Jane and I are so grateful for you kids, and for every Christmas we get to spend together. It's the highlight of our year, right here. Well, the left-over sandwiches we'll make with turkey tomorrow might be mine."

"I'll toast to that," Evan says. "Can't wait."

Holly has a soft look on her face. Warm and open. And in that moment I see what she sees. Christmas is a beautiful tradition for her. It's sugar and spice and family, not flavored with bitterness or expectations.

I see the world the way she sees it, and I want more of it in my life.

After dinner, Evan and Holly usher us all back into the dining room for the Secret Santa reveal. Her cheeks are flushed with color from food and eggnog, her eyes sparkling. "All right, everyone! It's the moment we've been waiting for all year! Is everyone ready?"

A chorus of yesses ring out and Holly gets a giant burlap sack with the words *Santa's Toys* cross-stitched on the side. It looks well-used.

I lean back in my chair and look around the room. Faces are open and eager, attention riveted on Holly as she hands out the presents using an old-timey broadcaster voice. Everyone gets one, including Winston, who has a giant red package set in front of him. He sniffs it with great interest.

"Oh, and we have one left... it's for Adam!" Holly says.

I set down my beer. "Pardon me?"

"This is for you," she repeats, handing me an elaborately wrapped gift. "Merry Christmas!"

I accept it. Run a finger over the wrapping paper. It has tiny penguins on it. "You shouldn't have," I say. "Whoever is responsible for this."

"You'll have to save it until you've correctly guessed who gave it to you," Jane says. She aims a warm smile my way. "Everyone coming to my house on Christmas will be included in the games."

"Thank you," I murmur.

I can't think of anything else to say.

Perhaps Holly notices that, because she directs everyone's attention away. "Let's get started!"

One after the other, members of the Michaelson family open their gifts and try to guess who in the family bought it for them. There's laughter permeating the air, and a sense of such good cheer that it's impossible to watch them without smiling.

"Golf clubs," Mr. Michaelson says. "This can only be from Evan. Right?"

Evan shakes his head. "Nope. Do you think I'd encourage it? You beat me too often the past summer."

Mr. Michaelson doesn't guess his wife until his last try, at which point she's covering her mouth to hide her grin.

I watch Holly closely when she opens her giant package. Her cheeks are rosy, her mouth a smiling slash of red. Her eyes widen when she sees what's inside. It's a fake Christmas tree, disassembled in three parts... but judging from the picture on the package, it'll be tall and full when it's put together.

"Wow," she says. Her hands fish around in the paper and pull out a tiny packet. It's Little Tree air fresheners, the ones you hang inside a car. "They're pine-scented. Oh my God. Evan, was this you?"

Her brother shakes his head. Holly's warm gaze travels one guest over, settling on his fiancée. "Sarah?"

"Yes," she says. "I'm sorry about my allergy. Evan told me that one of your favorite traditions is decorating the tree, and now you couldn't do that because of me. I thought—"

"No, no, please don't feel that way," Holly says. "I don't need a real tree!"

Sarah's cheeks are tinged with pink. "Well, I thought, maybe we could set it up tomorrow? Decorate it? I'd hate for you to have a Christmas without a tree."

Holly's eyes flicker to mine and I know what she's thinking. She already has a tree this Christmas. In my house. But the gesture is sweet, and in her eyes is love for her sister-in-law.

"Thank you," she says. "This is the best gift. I can't wait to put it up with you."

"I'm glad," Sarah murmurs.

Evan puts an arm behind her chair. "Hey, can I join this female bonding session?"

"If you ask *very* nicely," Holly says.

When it's time for Sarah to open her gift, the whole family is holding its breath in anticipation. I meet Holly's excited gaze. It's showtime for her.

Sarah pulls out a framed picture. "Oh, look at this. Is this you?"

Evan groans. "Yes. God, look at my hair. I don't want you to have these pictures."

"No, you look cute," Sarah says. "Oh! There's more!" She

pulls out the calendar of Fairhill's firefighters, the packaged snow globe, the neatly stacked recipes. The box is filled to the brim with bits and bobs from the town. I recognize the takeout menu from Dennis with some dishes circled in bright red pen. Evan's favorites, most likely.

Sarah looks across the room. "Holly?"

"Guilty as charged," she says. "It's a box with all of Fairhill. You know, a look into Evan's past. He can probably explain all of it."

He's already doing that. "You put in the recipe for Mom's meatloaf? Oh my God, you found the recording of my high school graduation!"

"Yup."

Evan and Sarah bend over the box, blond and brunette. Soon Jane and Craig join in.

I look over to Holly. "Great idea."

"Thanks for your help," she murmurs, smiling.

"I did nothing."

"Not true. You offered moral support during my snow globe shopping." She glances down at the gift on my lap. "You're next, you know."

I give her a withering look and she bites her lip to keep from chuckling. She knows exactly how much I hate all of this. And yet.. I don't hate it quite so much today. Not when I can see it from her perspective. It's the wildest of things.

The first present is a book. The cover is of a tropical beach with two illustrated people sitting in lounge chairs. A man and a woman.

It's called *The Vacation Affair* and it's very clearly a romance novel.

"Thank you," I say, confused as hell. "I've been meaning to read more."

Evan chuckles at my side. "Open it."

Inside is a Christmas card.

Merry Christmas Adam,

Sorry for pestering you about the Christmas lights. Welcome back to the street — we're happy to have you.

— The Maple Lane Book Club

Beneath are all the names of the Maple Lane ladies, including that of Martha Sanderson, the woman who had threatened me several times about the importance of uniformity in street appearance.

"This has to be from Jane?"

She nods. "The others thought it was a great idea, too. It's the book we'll read in January, although Martha suggested we look at your biography. The one that came out a few years ago?"

"Don't," I say. "It's filled with errors. I wasn't interviewed for it."

"Oh. Are they allowed to do that?"

"Unfortunately, yeah."

"Then we won't do that," Jane says. "I'll boycott it."

"Thank you, and thank you for this. Truly."

Holly chuckles across the table from me. "I think Mom wants you to join the book club. Giving you the next book is a pretty big hint."

"No, I know you're busy," Jane says. But her eyes sparkle. "You're of course very welcome to if you find the time."

"Mom," Evan protests.

"Don't *Mom* me," she says. "You know we've been trying to get men to join for years, but neither you or your dad are ever interested!"

"Because you read books like that," Craig says, nodding to the book in my hand.

I clear my throat. "Thank you very much, Jane. I'd be happy to, but I'll be moving back to Chicago in a few days. There's a New Year's Eve party I have to attend. Unfortunately it was scheduled months ago."

"Oh, that's a shame," Jane says.

"Have to get back to the office eventually," I say. "Besides, there are things there I can't stay away from."

Meaning one person in particular, and she's in this very room.

The others make polite humming noises at that. I can sense the curiosity behind it, but none of them have asked me about Wireout the entire evening. No one has made a comment about my life being anything other than perfectly normal. It must take effort, and it's not necessary, but damn if it isn't touching.

The night flows on. The family talks over one another in ways that are charming, conversations moving over memories and past Christmases like a dance. Evan is the attentive fiancé, always next to Sarah or explaining things to her in sotto voce.

Then the charades begin. The family is fiercely competitive, punctured by raucous laughter. Somehow I find myself acting out a popular movie in front of them all. Everyone has their eyes on me, except Winston, who is occupied with his giant jar of treats. It's ridiculous. It's also the most fun I've had in ages.

I sit next to Holly when I'm done. Our thighs touch, and my hand aches to take hers.

"Well done," she says.

I nudge her knee. "Don't patronize me."

She chuckles. "I meant it. Are you having fun?"

"I am."

"Liar," she murmurs. "But thank you for being here."

I bend closer to Holly. "I have something for you."

She looks around the room. The Christmas music playing softly in the background, the flickering light from the fireplace warming the room. No one is paying attention to us. "Outside the bathroom," she murmurs. "After charades."

We meet there later, with the family exhausted and talking quietly in the living room. She walks on careful feet to not jostle the bells of her Christmas socks.

We look at each other for a long moment. A slow smile spreads on her face, her cheeks flushed from laughter. "Hi."

"Hello." I kiss her. It's necessary after a whole day of seeing her but not being allowed to touch. She tastes sweet and a bit spicy from the mulled wine, like comfort and home.

She grips the collar of my shirt. "Thank you for coming. I know it can't have been easy."

I shake my head. "Don't thank me for anything," I murmur. "Not today. Not after everything you've done for me."

"Oh. Okay."

I glance over her shoulder. We're alone in the hallway with no one to see us. I take the risk and pull her into the bathroom, locking the door behind us.

"Adam?"

"I have something for you." I reach into my pocket. The tiny gift isn't nicely wrapped, but she doesn't seem to mind.

She turns it over in her hands. "You shouldn't've," she murmurs. She peels away the plastic to reveal a ceramic Santa from the Christmas Fair. "Oh my God. You got me drugs?"

"Maybe," I say. "You'll have to break it to find out."

She looks up at me. "Break it? Really?"

"Yes."

Holly turns the Santa around in her hands. There's a smile on her face. "I can't believe you actually want me to smash it."

"You're going to have to, to get the stash out." My heart is beating fast. This might have been too much, too fast. Too… weird. But it's too late, and all I can do is watch as she wraps her hand in a towel and gently taps the Santa against the porcelain of the sink.

I chuckle. "Put some force into it."

Holly smashes her hand down. The Santa breaks in three large shards, revealing the coiled piece of paper inside. I'd fiddled with the hole in the bottom to get it to fit.

She lifts it up with a crooked grin. "I'm not really familiar with drugs, Adam. What's this?"

"You're such a comedian," I say. "Go on, read it."

She unfolds the piece of paper and her eyes race across the line. It's a printout of an email from the editor-in-chief at the *Chicago Tribune*. I'd spoken to her at length when they interviewed me a few months ago, so it had been easy to send her an email last week.

To recommend a journalist to their investigative team.

Holly grips the porcelain lip of the sink. "Oh my God."

"It's just an interview," I say quietly. "They'll take a look at your portfolio. You could show them your piece about Fairhill, perhaps."

"Holy shit, Adam. You just emailed the editor and asked her for this?"

"Yeah." I run a hand over the back of my neck. Maybe I've overstepped.

But then Holly throws her arms around my neck. "You're insane," she whispers into my ear. "I can't believe you."

I grip her close. The warmth of her body molds against mine, her dress velvet beneath my hands. It feels so good to hold someone like this. A bit protective, possessive, like she belongs in my arms.

"Good surprise?" I ask into her hair.

"So much better than drugs," Holly says and wipes at her eyes. "You got me a shot at wowing the editor! Oh, I'm already nervous."

I grip her shoulders. "Don't be. You're a great writer."

"You haven't read anything I've written."

"Well, about that," I say.

"Adam?"

"I might have searched your name. I had to attach a few articles in my email, you know?"

She buries her face in her hands and I pull her close again, smiling against her hair. Holly's voice is muffled. "Please tell me you didn't choose the pimple-popping one."

"I didn't. I chose some great ones, about the changing media landscape, one you wrote when you were an intern. Don't worry." I tip her head back, meeting her eyes. For the first time in forever, hope is so strong it's like a pain in my chest. I want a future with her.

She brushes warm lips over mine. "Thank you."

"You're welcome," I murmur.

"I'm really happy you're here tonight."

"You are?" I lower my hands, gripping her curves. She's the real drug here. "Meeting the parents so soon... it's a big step."

She grins. "Yes. The whole family in one go. Did it scare you away?"

"Nothing would," I say, kissing the corner of her smiling mouth. "Besides, they seemed familiar."

She laughs. "I know they—"

"Holly? You in there? We're getting ready for the next round and I need you on my team."

"In a sec!" Holly says.

"Also, if you're laughing in a bathroom, you're doing something wrong," he adds through the door. "Weirdo."

"Mind your own business!"

I press my lips together to keep from laughing. The whole situation is ludicrous. I haven't seen Evan in years, and here I am, locked in a bathroom with his little sister in their parents' house on Christmas Day, my hands in places that are definitely *not* just friendly.

I wouldn't trade it for anything.

"I have something for you too," she whispers. She reaches into the neckline of her dress and gives me a tantalizing hint of a deep-red bustier, with lace. A blush is fierce on her cheeks. "Christmas-themed lingerie. It'll break your hatred of this holiday."

I close my eyes and breathe deeply through my nose. "Christ, Holly."

I can picture her in it. Shy and confident at the same time, eyes glittering, read lace hugging her curves. I want her so badly.

She presses a quick peck to my lips. "That's for later. Come on, I'll go out first." She unlocks the bathroom and peeks out. Only to find her brother leaning against the opposite wall.

He spots me behind her and his eyes widen. "Oh."

"Evan," Holly says. "You shouldn't wait outside bathrooms."

He looks from me to his sister and back again, the realization dawning. I step out and close the door behind us.

"We're dating," I say.

Holly looks up at me. "Wow."

I give her a crooked smile. "Cat's out of the bag, isn't it?"

"I didn't expect this," Evan says. His eyes are so similar to Holly's. They'd once been the mirror I held up to my own life. We'd been best friends back then, known one another so well. But it's been an eternity-long decade since then.

I brace myself for the worst.

Evan grins. "Hell, man. You move into your old house, and now you're dating Holly?"

"Yes. One was planned, but the other wasn't," I say carefully.

"Are you trying to relive something?"

"Hey," Holly says. "We've never dated before."

"Your brother would have beat me up back then if we had," I say. But I'm looking at Evan when I say it. Her family means everything to her. After eating dinner here as a kid, after seeing them today... I understand why.

There's a warmth here that would melt anyone's ice.

"Nah," Evan says. "I'm happy for you. Holly's one of the good ones, you know. Even if she's terrible at Monopoly."

"Untrue. I lost yesterday because of a rounding error."

"You mistook your hundreds for thousands and spent more than you could afford to," Evan says, reaching out to tug on a lock of Holly's hair. "Maybe you should get your eyes checked?"

A soft voice drifts from the kitchen. "Evan, baby?"

He straightens. "Right, Sarah wanted more mulled wine." He disappears down the corridor without a second glance at us. Holly sighs and pretends to wipe her forehead. There's glitter on her hand, leftovers from the gift unwrapping.

"Sorry about that," she says.

"I don't mind." I reach for her hand. It feels right in mine. "Should we tell your parents too?"

"We'd better. Prepare yourself, though. Remember what I said."

"Your dad will give me his blessing to propose," I say. "I remember."

Holly groans and I laugh, pulling her toward the living room. It's filled with laughter, a family's memories and traditions woven into a holiday that I still don't like... but that isn't so bad with Holly Michaelson by my side.

Epilogue

Holly

I rub my gloveless hands together. It's freezing, even inside the giant lobby, and I'm not dressed for the polar temperatures outside. But if there's one day a year where you can't think sensibly, it's New Year's Eve.

My dress is silver and sparkly and falls to my knees. Thin straps on my shoulders are the only things holding it up.

It had been an impulsive purchase.

Adam invited me to the New Year's Eve party he had to attend for work, but I already had plans. Dinner with my closest girlfriends from college.

Who, incidentally, thought I should go to my new boyfriend's party.

So I compromised. Arriving just before midnight will let us celebrate the new year together, which is perfect. But it also means showing up to a place where Adam isn't Adam-from-across-the-street, or even Adam-son-of-the-infamous-Dunbar. It's a place where he's Adam Dunbar, founder of Wireout, billionaire and genius. A world I've never seen him in.

A world I've never been invited to.

Sure, he'd groaned at the necessity of this party, saying he wished he could skip it. But the elevator I'm waiting for is gilded and the air smells like lilacs. Do they hide scented candles in the lobby? Install scent diffusers in the walls?

"Top floor, miss," an attendant says by my side. He's been all smiles as soon as I'd showed my invitation.

My butterflies get more and more active with each floor the elevator climbs. But I tell myself that Adam spent Christmas with my family. It's only fair that I see his work, essentially his adopted family, on New Year's.

The doors open and I hear them before I see them, the sound of a live band playing and the unmistakable mix of voices when a large crowd mingles.

I follow the sound, my heels click-clacking on the stone floor.

We're on the top of the Rush Hotel and the views of Chicago's skyline are breathtaking. We're surrounded by the city.

I pass a group of men in tuxes. Dressed to the nines for the New Year, and as I glance around, the cocktail dresses worn in this room could rival a catwalk. Adam had sounded like he'd rather be tortured than be here, but standing in this giant room, my eyes are like saucers. I understand why the invitation he'd given me carried so much weight.

The guests are here to mingle, to see and be seen, to celebrate New Year's Eve with people they considered their equals. If you had to donate to charity while doing it, well, that was a small price to pay.

I could write a great article about this, I think.

I try to look past the throngs of people, the cocktail tables, the live band, but I don't see Adam. The tiny straps of my heels dig into my ankles. I haven't seen him since we said goodbye in Fairhill. He'd driven back to Chicago two days before me, and we'd spent our last day together in front of the fireplace in his house.

The same way it all started.

I fiddle with the lock to my clutch and get it open. My phone reads eleven forty-five. Only fifteen minutes left until midnight. I've got to find him.

Then mic static rings out. The music quiets down, a hush spreading across the crowd. "Good evening, everyone," a deep male voice says.

It's familiar.

Adam is standing on the stage with a mic in hand. He hasn't

126

shaved his beard, despite threatening to do it back in Fairhill, and unlike most men here he isn't wearing a tux. Black suit, white shirt, no tie.

He looks comfortable up there. Wide-legged stance and a face that's impossible to read. This is him when he's back in his world. The man who was invited to give commencement speeches, cut ribbons, fund a new hospital wing.

The man who spent Christmas with me and my family.

"On behalf of the foundation, I want to thank you all for coming tonight. It means a lot that you would end the year with us, but even more that you're willing to begin the next one with us too. None of you got any better party invites, did you?"

Laughter rings out around the room. It's polite, eager. I don't know how he can stand everyone's attention like it's nothing. I would be a mess of nerves.

Adam looks out over the crowd, eyes searching. "We only have fifteen minutes left of the year. If there's anything left on your to-do list, I suggest you do it now. Otherwise, please grab a glass of champagne and donate if you haven't already."

His eyes find me, and despite the distance between us, they light up. I can see it. "The terrace offers the best view of the fireworks," he says, "for those who haven't brought someone to kiss. Happy New Year's Eve."

There's more polite laughter, people nudging one another. I only have eyes for Adam. He hands the mic off to an attendant and a giant screen blazes to life behind him. It's a countdown.

He steps off the stage and cuts a line straight through the crowd. They're watching him, and they split like the Red Sea around his advance. It's clear that he's the guest of honor here tonight. I hadn't realized that, not when he made it sound like a boring work event he had to endure.

Adam's eyes don't leave mine and my heart is beating fast. He's doing this in front of everyone, the guests, the reporters.

"Hello," he says, lips curving into a private smile. He presses a kiss to my cheek. I lean into it, into him, and feel his hand settle at my waist. "Thank you for coming."

"Of course," I say. It's hard to ignore people's stares.

His eyes travel over my dress. "You look gorgeous."

"Thanks. You look very handsome." My hand itches to run over his beard, but we're not in private. "You didn't shave."

"I didn't want to disappoint you."

"You could never," I say. But just imagining the raspy tickle against my neck as he kisses his way down my body is making me want just that.

He motions for a waiter and gets us two glasses of champagne. People have resumed their conversations around us, but they cast curious looks our way. He ignores them and leads me onto the terrace. It's built like a greenhouse, glass shielding us from the elements.

"This place is fancy," I say.

"Yeah, but it only has one purpose, and that's for functions like these." His hand is still on the small of my back. "I'm glad you're here."

"You've said that twice now," I tease. "Was it that bad before?"

"Unbearable. Dry food, boring small talk, these shoes give me blisters. Absolutely intolerable."

I grin. "That sounds awful."

He might be dressed up, imposing and venerated and in a suit I'm sure costs more than my used car, but he's still Adam Dunbar. Silly and himself and honest with me.

I lean against his side. "Well, my dinner party was amazing. No torture involved."

"Oh?" he says softly. "I'm glad."

"My friends are really curious about this mystery guy I'm dating."

"Mystery," he repeats. "You've only known him most of your life, you know."

"You're still a mystery," I say. "I don't know if you prefer coffee or tea in the mornings, which side of the bed you sleep on, what you wear to bed. What if I come over to yours this week and discover you sleep in a proper pajama set like an old English gentleman? With a hat and socks and everything?"

"You're ridiculous," he says. But he bends his head and speaks into my ear. "It's always coffee, my favorite side is the one you're on, and I don't sleep in pajamas. With or without a hat."

"Oh," I breathe. "Good to know."

"Will you spend the night at my place?"

"Start the new year right?"

His eyes are warm and heated on mine. "Yes."

"I'd love to. I might have even packed a toothbrush. Although I guess I shouldn't admit that, right? It makes me seem presumptuous."

He smiles again. "Very. My beautiful girlfriend wants to sleep with me. I'm offended."

Heat rushes to my cheeks. Girlfriend? We've only been dating for a few weeks, but it feels right. Like I've known him forever, and yet I can't wait to discover all the little things I don't know.

"You're blushing?" he asks, tipping my head back.

"You said girlfriend. Is that what I am?"

"If you want to be, yes."

I give a tiny nod, his hand still on my cheek. "I do. Very much."

"Then that's what you are." His thumb moves in a circle, sweeping along my jaw. "You're honest, sweet, funny. You spread magic, Holly. It touches everyone around you."

"Oh," I breathe.

"I might be obsessed by it. By you."

"That's okay. I… well, I might be completely, stupidly in love with you."

His lip curls. "Yeah?"

"Mm."

"Well," he murmurs, lowering his head. "I'm in love with you too. Little Holly Michaelson."

I open my mouth to protest, but he stops me instead. The kiss is achingly sweet. It makes me light-headed, so airy I might float away in this giant, domed building. He feels the same way. The knowledge feels like a gift.

Adam lifts his head and looks back at the crowded room. People have started to chant. *Ten. Nine. Eight.*

"Seems like I kissed you too early."

Seven. Six. Five.

I grip the lapels of his suit jacket. "That's okay. You can kiss me again."

Four. Three. Two.

"Thank God," he murmurs, and presses his lips to mine.

One. Zero.

Fireworks explode around us, coating the sky in vivid colors. But I hold on to the man of my dreams and kiss him back as fiercely as he's kissing me.

The future is bright enough already.

Epilogue II

Adam
One year later

"You okay?" Holly asks. She reaches across and puts her hand on mine, resting on the steering wheel.

I look away from my old house. It's decorated to the brim with Christmas lights, lit up like a beacon. "Yeah."

"How does it feel? Seeing them live there?"

"Good," I say, and I'm surprised to find I mean it. Renting out the house had been the right decision. Having it empty was depressing, not to mention a waste, and I don't want to live there. My return to Fairhill in those odd months last year had given me exactly what I'd sought, without knowing it. Closure and Holly. I couldn't ask for anything more.

"It's good to see new memories being made there," I say. "The tenants are a family with small kids, and this is a great neighborhood."

"They're really nice, too," Holly says. "Apparently Mom got Mrs. Sheen to join the book club."

That makes me snort. "Nothing ever changes on Maple Lane."

Her hand pats mine. "Not the things that matter, anyway. Ready to go inside?"

"Yes."

"It will be absolute chaos," she warns me. "Sarah and Evan have already arrived."

"Good. We owe them an ass-kicking in Monopoly after the last time we had them over for dinner."

She grins. "Have I ever told you I love you?"

"Yes. Often, and frequently. But I think I can endure it one more time."

"I love you," she says, leaning over the console to give me a quick kiss. "You treat board games with the seriousness they deserve."

"It's a respect thing, you know?"

Holly laughs and opens the car door. I follow suit, stepping into the cold Michigan air. Winter has a firm grip on this part of the country and it won't let go any time soon. I grab both her bag and mine, ignoring her protests. Her arms are full with the presents she'd lovingly wrapped the week before.

She's right, the house is chaos. It's warm and smells like baked bread and cinnamon, and Winston is a blur around our legs, wearing a pair of doggy antlers.

"I bought them for him," Sarah says. She's warmed up since marrying Evan the past summer, and Holly has found a true friend in her. They hug tightly in the hallway like they haven't seen one another for months.

Evan gives me a half-hug. "Was the drive okay?"

"Yeah. Had to take it slow for an hour or two, though. Ice on the roads."

"We had that too," he says. "Come on, let me get you a beer. I want to ask you about some investments I have lined up."

"Oh?"

"Yeah. Remember you told me about the new company out in Denver?" I follow him into the kitchen. Our old friendship is back. It's mature now, not based on video games or girls anymore. It's sports and family and work, running over a deep undercurrent of familiarity. He'd known me before I became who I am, just like I knew him before he became himself fully. That kind of bond is irreplaceable.

I didn't realize how much I'd missed it until I have it again.

Jane Michaelson interrupts her son by barreling past him and pulling me in for a hug. "You two made it."

I hug her back. "We did. Thanks again for having us."

"Anytime and all the time. No need for a holiday, even." She leans back, eyes twinkling. "How's your mother doing?"

"Great. We celebrated with her yesterday in Chicago."

"You know she's always welcome here if she wants to," Jane says. "It was great to see her again the past summer."

I nod. "Thank you. I know she appreciates that."

My mom's scars run deep when it comes to Fairhill, though, and our relationship was never what Jane's is with her kids. I envy Holly that, but I'm grateful for it, too. For what I've gained.

"Here, man," Evan says, handing me an opened beer. "Enjoy the peace and quiet while it lasts. Our aunt and uncle are coming down tomorrow and Sarah's parents will be here the day after."

I nod toward the living room, where music is playing, and Craig Michaelson is telling a story that makes Holly and Sarah laugh. Winston barks from the couch. "That's peace and quiet?"

Evan snorts. "It's all relative."

"Is everything good with your in-laws?"

"Yeah. The usual, you know," he says, but then he gives me an evil grin. "Or maybe not. You couldn't really tell me if you hated yours, could you?"

"I could, but it would be an unwise move," I say. I touch my beer to his. "Luckily I don't."

"You're allowed to be exasperated. I've heard Mom dropping hints about marriage. Sorry, dude."

I look over at the living room. The light from the plastic Christmas tree is gilding Holly's blonde hair, but it's her giant smile that shines the brightest.

"I've heard them." I think about the gift I'll give her this Christmas, and wonder what her answer will be.

<hr />

"All the times I was in this house as a kid," I say, "and I never thought I'd sleep in little Holly's bedroom."

"How does it feel?" She's sitting cross-legged on her barely-big-enough-for-two bed in her childhood bedroom. The walls are yellow, the coverlet crocheted by her grandmother. She's in her Christmas pajamas. Flannel shorts with reindeer on them and fuzzy socks. Her red T-shirt says *Gangsta Wrapper* above a pile of elaborately wrapped gifts.

"It feels like I'm doing something wrong," I say. "But also like I've finally managed to do something right."

Holly chuckles and runs a brush through her hair. It falls gleaming down her shoulder. "I get that. You know, if I'd known you'd one day sleep with me in here when I was a pining teenager, I would have freaked out."

"Come on, you never really *pined*," I say. "Did you? You never seemed nervous when we spoke."

She puts the hairbrush down with a wide grin. "Adam, you were the biggest crush of my childhood. I definitely pined. If they'd sold posters of you like they did of the Backstreet Boys, you would have been on these walls."

The compliment hits unexpectedly. She loves me now, and I never tire of hearing it. But knowing she'd cared that much for me back then makes my chest tighten. "Well," I say, and then can't think of anything else to say.

Her face is soft. Free of makeup and glowing. "You're not the one who's supposed to be embarrassed by that."

"I know. I'm not."

"Then what is it?"

I put a hand against the wall to brace myself. Is this the moment? It might be. It's not particularly romantic. But it's her and it's us and it's our past and our future colliding. I want to ask her so bad it's making me dizzy.

But what if she says not yet? Or worse, no?

"Adam? You're acting strange."

"I love you," I say. "More than I've ever loved anybody."

Her eyes warm. "Come here."

I close the distance between us and she pulls me down, softness and warmth, until I'm lying beside her on the narrow bed. Her hands grip my face. "I love you too," she says. Her voice sounds like a benediction. "I was thinking recently about how lucky I was when I came back here for the holidays last year. I hated the job I had then, I felt stuck, I wasn't dating… But then I met you again. What if we hadn't crossed paths?"

My hand curves around her hip and two fingers slip under the hem of her shirt, finding warm skin. They say you can't make homes out of human beings, but God help me, she's mine.

"Holly," I say. "I never want to live without you."

Her hand slides into my hair. "I don't want to either."

"I didn't know what I was missing before. How much better life could be with you in it," I say. "It wasn't just Christmas I hated before. I was… a cynic."

"Was?" she teases, but her eyes are warm on mine.

"More of a cynic, at any rate." I trace her bottom lip with my thumb. "I didn't know how much *life* I'd given up for my company before you showed me. Before you helped me reclaim it. This past year with you has been the best of my life, by a landslide. It's not even a competition."

She kisses me. It's so sweet it makes my chest ache. "What brought this on?" she murmurs. "You're not usually this expressive. I love it, don't get me wrong."

It's a split-second decision to do it now. I could wait, make it bigger, but that's not us. It's not me. It's not as real as this moment, when it's just the two of us and the togetherness we've built. It took trust and bravery on both our parts. I can feel my blood pounding in my ears, destiny waiting in the wings.

She's my future. I can only hope she'll let me be hers.

I slide my arm out from beneath her.

"Adam?"

"One second." I reach for my bag and the box. It's large and velvet and for a brief second of panic I wonder if she'll even remember, if she'll get the inside joke.

But love is always a leap of faith.

Holly's eyes widen when she sees the box. "Is that for me? Christmas is two days away."

"I know." I sit down next to her on the bed. She's in her pajamas, I'm in my boxers and a T-shirt, and it's eleven p.m. in her childhood bedroom.

And yet my throat feels so thick it's hard to get the words out. I hand her the box instead. "Wow," she murmurs, stroking the box. "How come?"

I put a hand on her knee, needing the soft feel of her bare skin to steady myself. "Open it, sweetheart."

She undoes the bow and opens the lid with a smile. "You're crazy. You already give me too—oh. One of Larry's ceramic Santas?"

"Yes," I say.

Holly's hand strokes the tiny thing before moving to the silver hammer beside it. Both inlaid in satin. "But we haven't been to the Christmas Fair yet. When did you get this?"

"I pulled some strings." It had taken a few phone calls with Larry to explain exactly *why* I wanted him to put a ring inside one of his creations, but once he understood, he had been an enthusiastic partner.

Holly narrows her eyes at me. "You got me drugs again?"

My chest loosens. She remembers. "Yeah. Thought it was time."

"How many grams fit into one of these?"

"Too many," I say, and then I need it over with, I need her to see the ring. I need to know her response. "Break it."

Her smile is delighted. "All right, and you even got me a hammer. Here I go…"

She brings the hammer down on the unsuspecting Santa staring placidly up at her. It breaks into a couple of shards on the velvet.

Revealing a platinum ring with a solitaire diamond.

"Oh," she breathes.

I can't think above the roaring in my head, but somehow I manage to sink down onto one knee in front of her. She's so beautiful, hair loose around her shoulders and in her Christmas pajamas. Vulnerable and real and soft and mine, I hope, for the rest of our lives.

"Holly," I say.

Her eyes well up and she gives a tiny, quick nod.

"You are the greatest thing to ever come into my life," I say. "I wish I'd realized that sooner, so that I could have spent the past decade with you, too. But I'll never stop being grateful that I came back to Fairhill and met you again. There are so few people in the world I'd decorate a Christmas tree with, sweetheart, but you're one of them. The only one."

She gives a hiccupping laugh and a tear spills over, racing down her cheek. I reach for the ring among the Santa wreckage.

"I want you to force me to put up Christmas lights on our house, to hog all the covers, to nag me into getting two rescue dogs. I want all of it, forever."

"I'm okay with just one dog," she whispers. Her voice is shaky.

"Holly," I say. "Will you marry me?"

"Yes," she breathes. "Yes, yes, absolutely. Yes."

"Thank God." I reach for her hand and slide the ring on her finger and then she's in my arms, crying against my neck. The velvet box is a hard weight between our bodies. Her heartbeat is as fast as my own.

I can't remember a single moment in my life when I've been this happy.

She leans back, wiping her eyes. "You got the ring *into* the Santa," she says breathily. "How did you do that? It couldn't have fit?"

"I might have made Larry an offer he couldn't refuse."

"You planned this for weeks," she whispers, looking down at her finger.

"Your dad helped me," I admit. "He went to pick it up."

"My dad?"

"Yeah. Gave me the blessing this summer, actually." He'd

done it unsolicited, just as she'd predicted, which had made me laugh.

Right after I'd thanked him.

"Adam, wow… We're engaged."

"Yes." I pull her into my lap on the bed, unable to stop touching her. Needing her close. "I know it's early. We've only dated for a year. But I don't need—"

"Me neither," she says. "Adam, I know what I feel. It's not going to change. Never, ever."

How did this incredible person become mine?

"My feelings won't either," I say. "If you want to have a long engagement, we can. But I couldn't wait to ask you. I wanted you to know how serious I am, how important you are to me."

She rests her forehead against mine. "Thank you. But I feel the same way. Wow. We're engaged. You're my fiancé."

"Yes."

"I love it," she whispers. "Already."

"You don't mind, then? That I proposed in your childhood bedroom in your parents' house?"

"No. This is where I pined for you, after all. Fairhill is where we met again last year. What could be more right?"

I kiss her, pressing her close. This beautiful woman who has turned my life upside down and somehow put it in order again. The house is silent, everyone in their respective bedrooms, so we have to be quiet. But there's no way in hell I'm not making love to my fiancée after I've proposed to her.

She presses her mouth to my shoulder to keep silent and I thrust slowly, afraid of the bed hitting the wall. But it's still some of the best sex we've ever had, fueled by our happiness. It grows between us until I nearly go cross-eyed with the pleasure and have to bury my face against her neck to keep from waking the house.

Holly lies in my arms afterwards, running her hand over my chest. I lift it up with my own and watch the faint light from her bed lamp catch on the diamond.

I chuckle.

"What?" she asks.

"I just realized that Christmas will now be the anniversary of this. Our engagement."

"Oh, you're right."

"Which means," I say, "that you've finally succeeded. It's now my favorite holiday."

She rests her cheek against my chest "I knew you'd come around eventually."

OTHER BOOKS BY OLIVIA
LISTED IN READING ORDER

New York Billionaires Series

Think Outside the Boss
Tristan and Freddie

Saved by the Boss
Anthony and Summer

Say Yes to the Boss
Victor and Cecilia

Seattle Billionaires Series

Billion Dollar Enemy
Cole and Skye

Billion Dollar Beast
Nick and Blair

Billion Dollar Catch
Ethan and Bella

Billion Dollar Fiancé
Liam and Maddie

Brothers of Paradise Series

Rogue
Lily and Hayden

Ice Cold Boss
Faye and Henry

Red Hot Rebel
Ivy and Rhys

Standalones

Arrogant Boss
Julian and Emily

Look But Don't Touch
Grant and Ada

ABOUT OLIVIA

Olivia loves billionaire heroes despite never having met one in person. Taking matters into her own hands, she creates them on the page instead. Stern, charming, cold or brooding, so far she's never met a (fictional) billionaire she didn't like.

Her favorite things include wide-shouldered heroes, late-night conversations, too-expensive wine and romances that lift you up.

Smart and sexy romance—those are her lead themes!

Join her newsletter for updates and bonus content.
www.oliviahayle.com.
Connect with Olivia

facebook.com/authoroliviahayle
instagram.com/oliviahayle
goodreads.com/oliviahayle
amazon.com/author/oliviahayle
bookbub.com/profile/olivia-hayle

Printed in Great Britain
by Amazon